"You ca[...] that g[...]" said. "And [...]

"She's got a point, you know," Abby chimed in.

Will took a bite of ice cream and smiled at me. "Come on, Whitman, don't be chicken. I'll take you. It'll be fun." Any other girl at Willow Hill would have fainted right there. But I couldn't see Will that way—he was just a friend.

Erin leaned forward and whispered under her breath, "It'll drive Sabrina insane if you go with Will." Sabrina, our archnemesis. The blond, beautiful queen of the school.

I don't know if Will knew that Sabrina liked him, but he heard what Erin said and didn't dispute it. In fact, his grin became even wider.

"Okay," I practically whispered.

"Yeah?" Will asked.

"Yes. It's a date."

CLAIRE RAY

Snow in Love

HARPER TEEN

An Imprint of HarperCollins*Publishers*

HarperTeen is an imprint
of HarperCollins Publishers.

Snow in Love
Copyright © 2009 by Claire Ray
All rights reserved.
Printed in the United States of America.

www.harperteen.com

Library of Congress catalog card number: 2008928090
ISBN 978-0-06-168805-8

Typography by Andrea Vandergrift
❖
First Edition

Snow in Love

Chapter 1

"So, my goal with your dress is total annihilation," my best friend, Abby, said as she pushed a large spiral-bound sketch pad across the table. "In other words, you will look so pretty that Sabrina Hartley cries. Anything less than actual tears and I'll count this as a failure."

I picked up the sketch pad and set my dish full of ice cream on the far corner of our table, where I hoped it would be less of a temptation. Not that I could keep away from it for too long. I mean, my family did own the ice-cream shop in town. There was only so much resisting I could do.

But for the moment my Chocolate Fiesta was forgotten. I was looking at the most exquisite, delicate dress Abby had yet to design. "Oh! It's so pretty!"

She grinned at me. "Really?"

"Really!" I smiled. "Only . . ."

"What?" she asked nervously.

"Nothing. Nothing. I just don't think my waist is that small." I pointed at the tiny midsection of the dress.

She ignored my comment and leaned over the booth's table, excited by her own vision. "It's going to be so beautiful! Look, I'll put two darts here, for a structured effect, and then the skirt is going to fall in white waves, so that it looks like a snowfall, see? I'm calling it my Princess Snowflake dress." Abby had always been something of a visionary. Where I'd see a routine high school class, she'd see a chance to learn something new. Where I'd see a regular Willow Hill boy, she'd see a handsome prince trapped in the halls of Willow High. Where I saw a pretty sunset, she'd she flames of romance.

Despite her ability to see things where I didn't, I trusted Abby more than anyone, and we were both determined that my dress at the Northern Lights Ball win the Annual Best Costume Contest, or as we called it, the ABC. The winners of the ABC won free ski passes for the Mount Crow Ski Resort. Which would mean that I could actually save the money I earned working at Snow Cones instead of spending it all on skiing. But the real reason that Abby and I were so desperate to win was so the Hated Sabrina Hartley would finally lose at something.

Our list of grievances against Sabrina Hartley was long. Sabrina had moved to our town of Willow Hill, Alaska, in the eighth grade. Right away she was annoying, because she was tall and smart and by far the prettiest girl in school. Her hair was unnaturally shiny—our friend Erin said she probably washed it in Crisco—and she was a *great* skier, the number one important thing to be in our town. (Her family had moved up here so her older brother could ski year-round at Mount Crow to train for the Olympics.) Sabrina was from *California* and let anyone within earshot know how much superior life in San Diego was to good ol' Willow Hill. But we hated her for more than just her better-than-us attitude. Her straight A's robbed Erin of her rightful title of eighth-grade vale-dictorian. And last summer she did something worse: She stole Abby's about-to-be boyfriend, Cam Brock.

Cam and Abby were next-door neighbors, and Abby had loved him from afar for years. (Actually, I guess she had loved him from up close. I mean, they *were* neighbors!) At the end of the last school year, it had seemed like Cam was finally noticing Abby; he'd asked her to go with him to the Spring Thaw Chili-Cook in Denali, and he'd been spending time at her house "studying." (Read: watching television and holding hands.) Then Sabrina set her sights on him, and bam! No Chili-Cook for Abby. Sabrina and Cam had been an item ever since. An annoying, nausea-inducing item.

Erin and I, to cheer Abby up, declared war on Sabrina, though really, we hadn't done anything except sneer at her. Our mission to rob her of the ABC crown was the first all-out assault we'd planned on her perfect life—what could I say? There wasn't a lot to do in Alaska. Revenge was a time filler. I was nominated for the role of prize-stealer because I was the only one of us with a boyfriend.

My eyes focused on the sketch Abby made

of my date, Jake. I could hardly judge men's clothes, but Jake would look so handsome in a tuxedo like she had drawn. Of course, Jake just happened to be the cutest boy I'd ever met, with brown hair that flopped irresistibly over his forehead, deep brown eyes, and one mole on his cheek that was *very* kissable.

"You're frowning. Why are you frowning?" Abby asked suddenly. Abby was a sensitive girl. I didn't even know I *had* been frowning and she'd picked up on it. "You're not happy?"

"No! Gosh, they're so beautiful. Totally crown-worthy." I reached for the dish of Chocolate Fiesta ice cream, my favorite. My mother made it by melting chocolate together with crushed hot pepper. Sounded gross, but tasted heavenly. "It's just, are you going to have enough time to make this? The ball is only two weeks away."

Her face pulled itself into a slightly surprised pinch. "Of course! All I need are your measurements. And Jake's so we can get his tux to fit perfectly."

At this I crammed a large, chilly bite into my mouth and peered around the inside of Snow

Cones, my family's shop. The bright red booths and vinyl-covered stools were empty, save for two freshman girls poring over fashion magazines at the ice-cream bar. The black-and-white tiled floor gleamed from the hard-core mopping my mother and I had done this morning. Once the sun began to set, there would be so many customers in here I'd barely be able to breathe. But now, it was quiet enough for me to lollygag with Abby and eat a little midafternoon snack. I glanced quickly toward the door, hoping Jake would walk through it. As I turned back around to face Abby, I pulled my cell phone from the pocket of my brown, extra-insulated corduroys. No messages.

Abby's face looked blatantly concerned, which made my insides do a little flip. "You'll have plenty of time to get measurements," I told her. Then I ate another bite of ice cream and looked down at the sketch. I just wasn't sure Jake would be here to make it to the dance.

Jake Reid didn't live in our town or go to our school but he'd been my boyfriend for three years, since I was a freshman and he was a sophomore. Jake's family owned one of the twelve pine-log cabins on the edge of the Mount Crow Resort. (His family's was the biggest, with a porch and a hot tub and a swing set.) Every year the Reid family arrived in Willow Hill the day after Christmas. They'd stay until the day after the Northern Lights Ball, and then they'd go back down to Juneau, and Jake and I would live on emails and texts until the next time we could see each other.

"Have you warned him about the dance yet? And the Make Sabrina Cry at the Ball campaign?"

"I'll fill him in when he gets here. He won't care about having to rent the tuxedo."

Abby looked down at the sketch and bit her lip. "I know, Jess. I'm just worried about clothing. We need to make sure he gets a normal tux, not some hideous discounted powder blue monstrosity."

Abby was lying. It wasn't the tux she was worried about; it was Jake. Erin had gone and planted a seed of doubt in her mind, the same seed she'd been attempting to sow in mine for the past week.

The fact was that I kind of hadn't heard from

Jake in about three weeks. We were usually in constant contact by phone or texts or IMs. Erin had gotten wind of the fact that there'd been a Jake blackout and was convinced that he was too chicken to tell me that his family wasn't going to be here for the break. Erin didn't like Jake. Two years ago he had promised to drive her to some ungodly depressing film festival in Anchorage — "Foreign Films by Foreign Females" — but had to cancel when his little sister broke her leg in an unfortunate tobogganing incident involving me and my poor steering ability. Ever since then, Erin claimed that Jake was wishy-washy, which was completely ridiculous. I mean, what better reason to cancel than a sister with a broken leg? But once Erin decided something, she never changed her mind. Which wasn't so bad except she always tried to prove her case to me. Her favorite examples were the time Jake bought two ski hats, one in blue and one in red, because he couldn't choose which color he liked best, and the time at the Mountain Diner where it took him so long to decide whether to order mashed potatoes or French fries that the waitress brought him both.

Erin just didn't get him, but I did. Despite his occasional bouts of indecisiveness Jake was one of the most caring people I'd ever met. He didn't like to hurt people's feelings, unlike Erin, who didn't really care what people thought of the things she said.

But Abby, who is the sweetest, most impressionable girl you could ever meet and whose heart had been trampled by Cam Brock, was beginning to wonder if Erin was right.

I carried my empty dish behind the counter and filled it with a generous scoop of Chocolate Fiesta. As I covered it with a dollop of whipped cream, I kept a close eye on the back doorway, making sure my mother didn't suddenly appear from her office and discover what I was doing. She hated when I "ate the profits," which I tended to do when I was feeling unsettled. I knew I shouldn't feel this way. Jake was a senior. He was probably busy with finals and college applications and things like that.

I licked some whipped cream off my pinkie finger, and pointed at Abby, who was still in the booth. "Abby! You and Erin have me thinking the worst!"

Abby's soft features arranged themselves into a smile. "I'm sorry, Jess. I just want your costume to be the best."

"It will be." I sat back down with her and perused the sketches. Jake and I were going to look amazing; I decided then and there to stop worrying and to start imagining how great it would be when Sabrina actually came in second place! Not that that would fix Abby's broken heart. The best I was hoping for was this: that Sabrina would be so upset she'd dump Cam, and he'd wake up and realize that it was Abby who should be his girlfriend. "I just wish you were going."

Abby scrunched up her nose. "Nah, I don't want to." She didn't want to have to spend the night watching Sabrina parade around on Cam's arm. I couldn't blame her. The sight of them together made me sick to my stomach and I didn't even like Cam!

Fortunately for Abby, there was plenty to do to keep her mind off her boy troubles. These three weeks were hands down the best of the year. Sure, the sun came up at ten and was down again by four thirty, but in Alaska you looked for reasons to celebrate and the winter break was one of them. No school for nearly three weeks! And the best thing was that the Mount Crow Ski Resort, which pretty much made up our entire town, was at its busiest this time of year. Normally Willow Hill was what I would call sleepy. Erin called it bleak and depressing. But for these weeks in winter, it was a happening, crawling-with-energy place. There were activities, like the Welcome to Winter Day After Christmas Faire and the Northern Lights Ball, and Mr. Winter let you take sled rides with his Iditarod dogs, and the hockey rink wasn't closed to all non-hockey-team skaters. It was what I imagined life to be like in the Lower 48 year-round.

Abby pushed her bangs away from her face. "I just wish Erin would let me make a costume for her, too."

"That will never happen." I giggled, and traced the edge of the dress Abby had drawn with my finger. In fact, Erin had refused to go to the dance unless Abby agreed to dress her up as a black snowflake.

The door to Snow Cones swung open just

then, the clanging of the bells making me jump. I hated those bells. They were loud and meant I actually had to *work*. I slid the remains of my ice cream to Abby and pushed myself out of the booth. But as I was standing, I saw that it was only Will Parker and Erin.

I looked immediately at Abby, to point out the fact that Erin and Will were together. Her eyebrows shot up, and her mouth formed an *O*. I had decided that only love would shake Erin from her black-cloaked funk. Will was sunny enough to overcome Erin's sarcastic nature, but he was the apple of almost every Willow Hill girl's eye. It was a long shot that he'd ever settle for dating just one, but I still held out hope, for Erin's sake. Not that she'd ever expressed interest, but still.

As Erin and Will walked through the door, I saw that they were both red-faced. They were sort of speed walking, not really running but moving fast while trying hard to *not* run. In fact, they looked like they were trying to avoid being noticed. And Erin looked funny. She had on a too-long, too old-lady-like bulky midnight-navy parka that I'd never seen before. It didn't really fit her, and not only that, her left arm was draped in front of it, as if she were holding something underneath the coat.

"Oh no." I didn't know what it was all about, but the two of them were each mischievous in their own right. When they got together, the havoc they could cause was untold. Like the time last month when they tried to make an indoor ice rink in the basement of Willow High.

"Shut the door!" Erin exclaimed, catapulting herself through the Snow Cones entrance and snagging the sleeve of the ridiculously puffy coat on one of the bells. "Argh!" She made an odd sound as she tried and then successfully disentangled herself from the door.

"How do you lock this thing?" Will Parker fumbled around the door, looking for a lock.

"Hey, Will," the freshman girls sitting at the bar cooed. Will straightened up, forgetting whatever had been so urgent just moments before, ran a tanned hand through his sun-streaked hair, and flashed the smile that melted hearts up and down the halls of Willow High. "Hello there, ladies."

I rolled my eyes and Abby giggled.

"Will! Lock the door!" Erin half shouted through gritted teeth. Will looked at the door like he'd never encountered one before, so I casually walked over to where he stood and put my fingers on the lock, which was plainly above the doorknob.

"Oh," he said, turning his grin on me. "I don't know why I didn't see that."

Erin grunted her annoyance, teetered over to us, and pulled me by the sleeve of my shirt back toward the booth where Abby waited, puzzled.

"Will Parker, you unlock that door right now!" The booming voice of my mother came trumpeting in from the back room, and the four of us froze. My mother is a tiny woman, five one in sneakers. But she's all-knowing and all-seeing and can be a little bit intimidating.

"How does she do that?" Abby whispered while I shouted, "He didn't lock it, Mom, I promise!"

"If any customers can't get in because of you kids, you'll be manning the booth tonight, all by yourself, all night!" My mother never issued empty threats, and she knew very well that I'd rather do homework than have to work the booth at the Welcome to Winter Faire.

"It's unlocked, Mom!" I shouted again while Will and I ran to the door and each fumbled with the lock. I pushed his hands away finally and he looked at me sheepishly and mouthed the word *Sorry*.

"Will, you'll have to keep an eye out. Stand there and keep watch," Erin ordered. Her black hair tumbled down her back as she whipped off her dark gray hat. The black color of her hair came from a bottle. Naturally, it was as blond as Abby's, though she did look kind of striking this way.

"Keep an eye out for what?" Abby asked.

"What's going on? Whose coat is that?" I asked suspiciously.

Erin nodded her head and pointed a finger at me, an acknowledgment of my observation. "It's Mean Agnes's. I had to take it. It was the only coat bulky enough to hide it."

"Oh God." Abby put her head in her hands.

"You didn't." I said ominously as I sank

slowly to the booth's seat.

Erin pointed at Will. "It was his fault! He made me take it."

"Hey! You thought she should see too," Will said lazily from his post at the door. He never got excited about too much.

"Yeah, but I wasn't the genius who had the idea of *stealing* it. Do you know what Mean Agnes will do to me if she realizes what we did?" Mean Agnes was Erin's boss at the front desk of the Mount Crow Resort Hotel. She had it out for Erin, ever since Erin got caught lecturing some hotel guests about vegetarianism and how meat was murder. Agnes was old—nobody knew how old—and feisty. She hated all kids generally, and mouthy ones especially. Which was why she hated Erin.

"I was just going to have you come over. But it turns out that Will's a klepto." I didn't say anything to Erin, but if Will was a klepto, why was the stolen item in *her* stolen jacket?

"Erin! It's her! It's Mean Agnes!" Will pointed through the door, and Abby and I held our breaths while Erin tried to disappear beneath the table. Then Will shook his head and said, "Nope. My bad. Just a big dog there."

Erin glared at him.

"Guys, you're making me nervous," I said. "What's going on?"

"Sit down, Jessie," Will suggested.

"Yeah, sit here." Erin pointed at the booth seat across from her. "Like I said, this wasn't my idea." She unzipped the big bulky parka as Abby admonished, "I can't believe you stole her coat."

Erin snorted. "That's the least of my worries. Mean Agnes'll have a coronary if she finds *this* missing." And Erin produced a large, leather-bound, oversize volume from beneath the folds of the mammoth coat. She plunked it onto the table.

"You stole the Mount Crow register book?" I asked incredulously.

"Well, it serves Mean Agnes right for not letting us get a computer. We're the most exclusive resort in Alaska, and she's running it like it's the Middle Ages!"

Abby put a hand on Erin's arm, to calm her.

Abby is very soothing, and once Erin starts ranting about Mean Agnes, there's no slowing her down.

"Okay, so what do I need to see?"

Erin took a deep breath.

"Just show her already," Will shouted as a group of skiers walked through the door.

"I'll be right with you," I said to the customers as they approached the ice-cream counter. It would take them a while to pick what they wanted. My mother always made sure there were at least seventy flavors a day to choose from, from Almond Apricot to our house specialty, Zebra Stripe, which had chocolate and vanilla ice cream in a striped pattern.

"Hurry up, okay? My mom is going to kill me."

Erin took a deep breath again and flipped open the pages of the book. It was no easy feat. That book was old and dusty and probably weighed twenty pounds. From my vantage point across the table, I could see neat rows of old-lady-like penmanship, a list of names, check-in dates, checkout dates, and numbers of parties.

"I found it this morning. I didn't know what

to make of it." She flipped toward the back, to the list of entrants in the Northern Lights Ball. She put her finger on a pair of names and rotated the book so that I could read it.

I saw my own name next to Jake's. "There *you* are," Erin stated matter-of-factly as Abby's face grew more and more red. Abby hates suspense. She's too emotional to handle it. She always reads the last pages of a book first, she'll never go to a movie unless she knows the ending ahead of time, and she can't stand reality television because of all the "confrontation," as she puts it.

"Yeah?" I asked impatiently. I was getting bored with the cloak-and-dagger business, and I could see from the corner of my eye that our customers were ready to order.

"Will!" Erin commanded. "Take care of them." She pointed at the customers.

"Erin! He can't do that. Just show me."

Erin looked at me solemnly, then flipped the book to the next page. Her finger plopped on another name.

"Evie Stewart? Who's that?" I asked.

"Keep reading."

I did. Evie Stewart, of Boise, Idaho, was entering the Northern Lights Ball Annual Best Costume Contest with Jake Reid. My boyfriend. I was too confused to say anything. I looked up at Erin, hoping she could help me figure out what I was supposed to be thinking.

"He's here, Jess," Erin said sadly, and flipped back toward the front of the book. "His family got in yesterday." She pointed to another row of names in the register. Reid. Arrived yesterday at ten in the morning.

Jake had been in town for an entire day and he hadn't called me. And he'd brought another girl with him.

Chapter 2

The Welcome to Winter Day After Christmas Faire is the best night in Willow Hill, Alaska, hands down. The second greatest night in Willow Hill would have to be Christmas Day, because of the Angel Parade. This isn't your typical Christmas pageant. It's a parade on skis. Nearly every adult in town straps on a pair of boards and skis down the main hill of the resort dressed as an angel. It's a beautiful sight to behold, dozens of angels floating down the snowy mountainside. When they get to the bottom, there's apple cider and hot chocolate, and then everybody has a snowball fight. I've never been able to figure what a snowball fight has to do with Christmas, but it's a lot of fun, especially when Sabrina Hartley is close enough to pelt. Normally I can pay my little brother, Brian, to full-on assault her along with his other victims. That way she has no idea that she's being targeted at all, and if she did, she'd never think to trace it back to me. She probably doesn't even know I have a brother.

Anyway, the Welcome to Winter Faire had always been my personal favorite, even though there's no Angel Parade. It marked the beginning of the main tourist time here, which was my favorite not only because it meant Jake-time but because out-of-towners were good for breaking up the monotony of life. I mean, all the same kids had gone to my school since I was in kindergarten (except for Sabrina, who didn't count). There was nothing to do here but ski and ski and skate and then ski some more. So a few new faces made for a nice change of pace.

The Faire was always held at the resort, in the basin formed at the feet of three of the mountains. There were sled races and skating on the stream behind the two bunny hills and cross-country runs through the pine trees at the edge of the resort. The ski instructors and professional snowboarders from the area would give demos — Will's demo was always something to see: He would flip and float in the air like a bird in flight and the crowd was always huge because it was well advertised that Will had been on ESPN at the Winter X games.

In the basin itself, there were dozens of booths and stalls selling food, clothing, crafts, and other oddities. Mean Agnes recruited her employees—Erin, chief among them—to decorate the area with white lights, blue-and-silver decorations, strung-up cranberries, and large bales of hay. My dad landed the smallest of his planes at the south entrance of the resort, and for five dollars, he took kids up to circle the bay. My mother went all out for the Snow Cones ice-cream stall. She would make a special Welcome to Winter ice cream (vanilla, star anise, and blackberries—I'm not supposed to share the recipe). Old Man Jones, who lives about a mile from our house off a dirt path that is unmarked and can't be found by anybody who hasn't lived in Willow Hill their whole life and knows the woods without needing a map, came down from his yurt in the woods and whittled gifts. I had a handmade sign that said JESSIE SLEEPS HERE hanging above my bed. Last year he whittled a heart with our initials in it for me and Jake, and then he sawed it into two pieces, one of which I kept in my locker at school.

Normally I look forward to this day all year. Abby, Erin, and I plan not only our outfits, but the order of stalls we visit, what we are going to buy, how long we're going to ice-skate, whether we're going to enter the three-legged cross-country skiing contest (it's a sordid affair, really), and which of the sledders we'll root for in the races at the foothills by the stream.

But this year I wasn't all that excited. In fact, I was upset. The whole mess with the book was weighing on me. After my mother let me leave Snow Cones, I went straight home and called Jake's cell phone three times. He didn't answer. Then I called Jake's cabin three times. Again, nobody answered. I sent two text messages. No answer. The silence became loud.

I tried to calm myself down by whipping up my special Jessie Whitman Cheer-up Shake. It wasn't working. In fact, it was making me more anxious, both because of the sugar involved (it's an elaborate concoction featuring rocky road ice cream and Oreos and coconut; made correctly, it'll make your teeth hurt for two days at least) and because I was standing outside in ten-degree weather and the ice cream was freezing my insides.

I drank the last bits of the shake and looked around at the beginnings of the Faire. The people had begun to stream in. From where I stood in my mother's booth, I could see my dad climbing out of the cockpit of his canary-yellow-and-white plane. About a hundred yards from that was the stream where little kids, including my brother, Brian, skated in delirious circles, playing ice tag. Skating reminded me of Jake, of last year, when we held hands and spun each other around on the slippery surface of the stream until we fell down. I scraped my hand and Jake got a bruise on his chin, but we were laughing so hard we didn't even feel it.

I took a deep breath and dumped three scoops of rocky road ice cream into the large, metal shake-container I had just emptied. There was nothing else to be done. I was going to have to drink Cheer-up Shakes until I was cheered up.

Even after Erin had showed me the book,

I had trouble believing that Jake could be in Willow Hill already. Jake just wasn't that kind of guy; he wasn't like Cam Brock, who had lost interest in Abby overnight. Jake was sweet, he was good-natured. He opened doors for me when we went places, he made Abby laugh. He wasn't like Will Parker either, who had girls tripping all over themselves to date him but who was more interested in his latest snowboard or how many inches of snow we were going to get.

I reached underneath the table to the box where my mom had packed all the fixings. I grabbed two chocolate chip cookies, and crushed them into my shake-container. This kind of romantic worry called for a secret ingredient.

"Jess!" I looked up out of my reverie to see Abby and Erin walking toward me. Living in Alaska, getting dressed up means wearing your newest flannel shirt and a pair of clean jeans over thermal underwear. That's why Abby has always been a girl to admire. In twenty-degree weather (and that's in May!), she has always been able to dress fashionably, as if she were a Lower 48-er rather than a born-and-bred Alaskan. Right then, Abby was bundled up like a light-blue bunny rabbit. Her ski jacket was puffy and sparkly, and there was white fluff from the lining of the hood framing her face. Her cheeks were cherry-apple red and her eyes sparkled. Erin, on the other hand, was in dark gray and black from head to toe. In the dusky starlight—it was only six thirty, but dark enough to seem later—you could barely make her out. She liked to hide, she said, and wearing black all the time helped her do that. She didn't look happy. In fact, she was hopping back and forth between her feet, trying to keep warm.

"How can you be eating ice cream tonight?" Erin asked as the two of them approached the Snow Cones booth.

"Oooh, it's pretty!" Abby exclaimed, pointing to the red-and-white crepe paper decorations my mother had hung from the loose wooden framework my father had installed in lieu of a ceiling. "Mrs. Whitman," she called out to my mom, who was carrying a big heater over from the car. "It's so warm and romantic in here!"

I ran to help my mother with the heater, and

once we got it plugged in my mother turned to look at us. "Here you girls go." She handed me a twenty-dollar bill. "Now go. Have fun."

I bit my lip. Erin looked at me plainly. Normally it was Abby who could read my every feeling, but Erin had special radar for sad emotions. "Are you sure you want to wander around tonight?"

"Go," my mother pronounced. "No working for you." She kissed the top of my head and pushed me around the counter. "I mean it."

I could hardly argue with her. Once my mother said to do something, you did it. My mother and father grew up here in Alaska. Her father died in a silver mine when she was thirteen. My father's plane went down in the mountains by the Arctic Circle once when I was about six, and he lived for four days without anything to eat and only mountain snow for water. In short, they know a bit about dealing with hardship. So even though I had explained everything to my mother over dinner, about Erin and Will and the stolen book, and how Mean Agnes's handwriting looked like the spindly writing of the devil, and about how it seemed like Jake had already arrived without calling me, my mother didn't see any reason for me to be hiding out.

"Come on," Erin said, linking her arm through one of mine. "The best thing to do is to pretend like there's nothing wrong."

"Nothing is wrong," I said. "He probably just hasn't had a chance to call me yet."

"That's what I think," Abby chimed in. "Come on, let's go walk through the paper snowflake forest." All of us conveniently neglected to mention the mystery that was "Evie," but I like to live in delusion every now and then.

The forest was a tradition—every year people from all over the area contributed paper snowflakes. This may sound silly, but people don't have a lot to do up here, so the snowflakes get pretty creative. Last year there was an entire section of flakes made from doughnuts and cooked macaroni, and Brian got in trouble for eating them. They hung down from the same sort of lattice my father had made for our booth. Erin's favorite thing to do was to run through the forest, screaming. I kept wondering if we were getting too old to run screaming through feet of hanging paper art, but Abby and Erin were already half running to get there.

So I decided to just follow them. I wasn't normally a girl who let my imagination get away from me, and I'd spent an entire afternoon imagining Jake either dead in a ditch or wrapped around a creature named Evie. It was exhausting. And the shakes weren't working. Maybe playing with my friends among pounds of papier-mâché would do the trick.

"Keep drinking that shake, you'll have to enter yourself in the Northern *Fat* Ball."

The three of us stopped dead in our tracks. Erin was the first to whirl around, and Abby followed close on her heels. They stepped up to my side, and together the three of us faced our nemesis, Sabrina Hartley. Of course, only Sabrina would come up with a joke that wasn't even remotely clever or funny.

Sabrina had her two henchmen with her, Stephanie Bright (Erin called her S-Brat behind her back) and Hannah Landon. Sabrina was a monster of a girl. Taller than most boys in our class, with a loud voice and long hair. Everything about her just seemed bigger to me. When my mother first saw her in the parking lot of Willow High, she assumed she was a student teacher. She was a bully. She kept Stephanie and Hannah on a tight leash. If one of them liked something, Sabrina always either liked it more or first. And she treated Cam like a lapdog, always hurling orders at him, especially if Abby was close enough to hear them.

"Shut up, Sabrina," Erin snarled at her.

"Erin, you need to seriously invest in a few pastels. You look like the devil's messenger," Sabrina shot right back. S-Brat and Hannah just tilted their heads toward her and snickered.

"What do you want?" I asked her, seething.

"Well, the girls and I are headed over to the stream for skating. You're not going there, are you? We're afraid that if you're there, the ice will break."

I narrowed my eyes at her. "You're the giant freak, not me."

"Well, at least I'll have a date for the ball. You'll be disqualified, and your"—she pointed at Abby—"*dress*"—she pronounced it like it was a dirty word—"will have to be laughed at another time." With that, she flipped her obnoxious hair and stalked off through the trees, telling her minions loudly that only poor people made their own clothes.

"She's not even making sense anymore," Erin snorted.

Abby was sadly quiet.

"Come on, Ab," I cajoled. "She's just mean because she hates being stuck up here in Alaska."

"Yeah," Erin joined in. "Don't you know we're in exile up here?" She adopted a snooty voice, like a Hollywood starlet. "'Dah-ling, did you know that in San Diego the roads are made of *chocolate*?'" This made Abby smile, and then, because I wasn't focused on making Abby smile anymore, I started to feel worried.

"So, now can we run through the snowflakes?"

Erin asked the two of us.

"Erin, why would Sabrina say that?" I asked.

"Huh? I thought we just covered this. She's mean."

"No, I know that. But why would she say that about me being disqualified for being single? Why would she say that?"

Erin and Abby both looked at me and said nothing. Erin lifted her shoulders and pushed me forward. "She's just mean, that's all."

I walked along, slipping back into that queasy state I'd been in since seeing Jake's family name in the book. I reached for my cell phone, which was in the front pocket of my coat. Still no messages.

So I paged through the messages I had sent him. As I looked at them, checking to see how desperate they sounded, I began to sift through yesterday's, then the day before that. I went all the way back a week. I hadn't sent more than I usually did, and nothing I wrote could have been construed as naggy or needy, which my mother was always drumming into my head.

"Be your own woman!" she'd pronounce. "They tell you nobody will buy ice cream in Alaska, you laugh at them and open a store!" Then she'd cross her arms and nod her head and whatever worry I had would be an officially closed topic.

"Hey, you still with us?" Erin asked, knocking on my hat to be funny.

"Yeah, yeah. I'm here."

Abby took my shake from me and finished it off.

"This is so silly. If he wanted to break up, he would have told me, right?" I turned to Erin for confirmation. The answer to this question seemed kind of dire, and she was my go-to girl for that sort of thing.

"I don't see why not. Or he would just not come this year," she muttered.

"Thanks a lot."

"What? I'm just being a realist."

"No, he's here," Abby said with a squeak, stopping dead in her tracks. Erin and I looked at her in confusion.

"Huh?" Erin asked.

Abby didn't respond. She just raised her

arm and pointed into the snowflake forest.

Standing not twenty feet away from us was a couple hugging and laughing and kissing. It was Jake, hugging a girl as blond and tall as Sabrina.

Chapter 3

"*L*et's go." Abby tugged on the sleeve of my corduroy coat. Her face was framed in the fluff of white lining and shiny blue parka.

"No way. We've got to go talk to him," Erin countered.

My cheeks burned. My insides churned. My stomach felt like it was on the ground with my toes. My eyes were tingling, not with tears, but with that same sensation I got after a long night of reading or studying or wearing glasses. And the sound of my heartbeat flooded my ears. I felt like I was stuck in time. My feet wouldn't move, neither toward him nor away from him.

The two of them, Jake and this girl, were standing in the middle of the snowflake forest. He was mostly hidden by the large white paper flakes, but I could see *her*. She was tall and blond and excessively smiley. Her clothes looked expensive—she wore camel-colored pants and a pair of UGGs. I self-consciously crossed my arms to hide my own shabby-looking olive-green corduroy coat. I felt suddenly the same way I did at school in the presence of girls like Hannah and Stephanie, like I had missed a memo on how to dress.

"Come on, Jess," Abby said gently.

"Abby! She can't *run*!"

It was Sabrina who finally shook me from the wrinkle in time I was experiencing. I don't know if she and her henchmen were following me or what, but they appeared just in time to witness my shame. Sabrina stood right next to me, and I could feel her laughter in every corner of my body. "Wow, who's that, Jessie?"

"Shut up, Sabrina," Erin commanded, and pulled me away from her. I could hear the three of them cackling as they walked away and this only added to my feeling of confusion.

Then Jake clutched the girl's hand, and suddenly all the confusion I felt transformed instantaneously to sharp, bright anger. I couldn't help it. There Jake was, right here in Willow Hill, smiling. Cavorting. HOLDING HANDS. Here I'd been spending hours convincing myself that there was nothing wrong, and the whole time, there was a big something wrong! And it was BLOND!

Jake dropped the girl's hand and bent to pack together a medium-sized ball of snow. As he straightened, the dimples that he gets when he smiles were clearer than anything. Suddenly I was moving forward steadily, like a grizzly bear stalking for fish. Erin and Abby were right behind me, I could sense them. All around us little kids were shrieking and streaking through the snowflakes, which hung at different heights, some waist high, some right at head level. I pushed my way through, all the while looking at Jake and this girl.

Jake threw the snowball in her direction and she dove headlong into a thick section of paper snowflakes. He stooped to pack together another snowball and chased her. They bobbed and weaved through the flakes, throwing snow-balls at each other and laughing. The girl was beautiful. Striking. Her eyes were green and her skin shone a bright copper color. This was something you never saw in Alaska, a girl with this kind of tan. This said to me that she wasn't from here, and then I remembered what had been written down in the book—Boise, Idaho. They had sun enough there to tan you like this? I was being silly; you could get a tan everywhere, even in downtown Willow Hill. Mean Agnes's niece ran a tanning salon. My mother went there once and came back looking like a burnt cookie.

I marched forward and nearly lost my head to a snowflake. As I pushed it out of the way, I got a nasty paper cut on the palm of my right hand. "Ouch!" I tore the snowflake down. I recognized it—it was the one my brother, Brian, had made, complete with spikes. Great. Watching him make it, I had known that somebody would pay the price for his typical twelve-year-old fascination with warfare. I looked quickly behind us, hoping that Sabrina was within throwing distance.

Erin said quietly, "What are you going to do?"

Abby chimed in, "I think we should go."

I kept walking, until there was only three

feet between me and them. And then I stood there, quietly observing their glee. I didn't know the answer to Erin's question, I hadn't thought about what I wanted to accomplish. I guess I just wanted to see for myself that it was indeed Jake and not some evil twin who had taken over his body.

The two of them didn't notice me right away. They kept hurling snowballs at each other and giggling and shouting, until Erin said out loud, "Um, hello!"

This got their attention. The girl turned toward us, with a confused look on her face. A snowball dropped out of Jake's hand as he recognized the sound of Erin's voice. His dimples disappeared and he bit his lip. This was what he did when he got nervous. Like before the two of us would race down the double-black-diamond hill at the resort. Or the time we were hiking and came right into the path of a moose and her baby.

"Hey," I finally managed. As soon as I spoke, half the steam I had gathered in my march to where they stood leaked out of me. I normally wasn't a very angry sort of girl, and now that

I was this close to him, I started to feel things other than anger. I wanted to talk to him. And despite everything, I had missed him, and there was a part of me that was *really* glad that he was here.

Jake didn't say anything. He just looked at me. My eyes widened and I laughed a little bit. Abby moved in closer to my side.

Erin was the one who broke the tableau. "I'm Erin, and this is Jessie and Abby," she said to the blond, green-eyed girl.

"Hiya!" the girl exclaimed sweetly, brushing her snowy hands down the front of her gorgeous, green, flower-embroidered coat. It looked like it cost about five times as much as my coat did. "Are you guys friends of Jakey's?" She looked at him for an answer.

"Jakey?" Erin snorted.

I shot her a look both to quiet her and also to confirm that referring to him as "Jakey" was completely ridiculous. I'd never heard anybody call him that, even his mother.

But he didn't say anything to correct her. Instead he took a giant step away from her. I could hear the sound of crunching snow beneath his boots. He mumbled, "Yeah. This is Abby and Erin. And Jessie." That last part, the part about me, he completely swallowed into his throat. You could barely hear him. I stared at him hard, while he studied something interesting on the ground.

"We introduced ourselves already," Erin snapped. He looked at her quickly, then turned his head away again.

I don't know if the girl even noticed how awkward the moment was, or how mean Erin sounded, or how quiet Abby was, or that Jake's neck was turning a creepy shade of orangey-red, or that I was sweating a little bit too much for the mid-twenties Alaskan temperature.

Then, something hit me on the back of the neck with a *thwack*. My head snapped forward as I recognized the icy sting of a snowball. "Ow!" I screamed. More like bellowed. I couldn't help myself. It was entirely not cute or ladylike at all.

I whipped around to see who had released the offending missile, ready to stab Sabrina Hartley through the heart with my brother's snowflake if I had to.

"Sorry!" Will Parker pushed aside a

snowflake to see who he'd hit. He was holding a snowball in his other hand; it was poised in the air as if he were about to hurl it. "You okay, Whitman?" Two of his friends appeared at his side, Cam Brock and Jason Mitchell, this guy who used to go to our school but who was now in his second year of college in Anchorage.

Cam saw who Will was talking to and shoved his hands in his pockets. "Hey, Abby," he said, more to the ground than to her.

"Hey, Cam," she said quietly, also to the ground.

"Oh please no," Erin muttered. I felt bad for her. This had to be the worst meeting of people in the history of the world. I'm sure she didn't want to have to take care of *two* basket-case friends.

"Sorry about that." Will laughed as he trotted over to me. "Thought you were Brock," and with that he flung the snowball he was holding right at Cam's face.

"Hey!" Cam said as he got hit in the side of the head. It left a mark. Abby giggled in delight.

Will touched my arm. He was wearing a

navy knit cap with a pair of goggles resting over it, and the white snowsuit he'd worn last year at the Winter X games.

"That really hurt!" My voice was really — and I mean *really* — loud. Too loud. I was screaming at Sabrina and the tan girl and Jake all in one, and poor Will got the brunt of it.

"Whitman," he said, oozing the kind of charm that got him out of homework assignments and into the movies without having to pay, "I know you can handle a tiny little snowball." He smiled in a way that just irritated me and despite my intentions to retain *some* dignity, my eyes got a bit teary. That wiped the grin off his face.

Erin gritted her teeth. "Good work, genius," and nodded backward to Jake. That seemed to get through Will's easygoing, snowboarding skull. His face immediately changed.

"Are you okay?" the tanned girl asked me.

"Um, yeah, I'm okay. It was just a, um, a snowball." I don't know why I answered her. I was just so discombobulated by the whole exchange; I wasn't even clear on what the rules were. Was I supposed to not talk to her? What did one do in a situation like this?

"I never knew how much snowballs could hurt until today!" she responded empathetically. She was like a cheerleader, all sprightly and happy and cheery. I hated her. Then she stooped down, gathered together a snowball, and whipped it at Jake's legs.

"No!" Jake tried to stop her but it was too late. He had to jump to avoid being hit.

"I'm Evie, by the way," she said to us.

Will, who was late to the party, began to introduce us all, again. "I'm Will, and this is Cam and Jay. And this is Er —"

"Erin, Abby, and Jessie, I know." The girl grinned. I had a feeling that she was a girl who was hard to hate. Which made me hate her even more. "So Jake was telling me that you guys live here year-round. I can't believe that! You must have fun all the time. Look at this place!" And she spread her arms out at her side and did a little spin. "I feel like we're at the North Pole or something!"

Cam and Jay gave each other a look, and

Erin narrowed her eyes. Even among people she liked, cheeriness annoyed her.

I couldn't take it anymore. "Jake."

He exhaled deeply. "I'll call you later, okay?" he said under his breath.

Evie, the tanning goddess, heard him and mistook his meaning. "Yeah! That'd be fun! Can you guys hang out with us later?"

"Um. No," Jake said. "I mean, they probably have stuff to do."

"No, act—"

"We do, actually," Erin interrupted me. "*Right*, guys?" she said this part to me, Will, Cam, Jay, and Abby.

I knew what she was trying to do. She was trying to salvage my self-respect, which I was too upset to do on my own.

Fortunately Abby knew all about self-respect and how much you missed it when it was gone, so she stepped up to me and threaded her arm through mine. "Yeah, it was good seeing you, Jake. We've got to get going."

Then Will got in on the act. He nodded his head and said a little too loudly, "Okay, Whitman. We'll see you guys tonight."

Erin gave him a condescending look, and he raised his shoulders to let us know that he was trying to help.

And with that, Erin and Abby ushered me away from Jake. I was crying before I could even get to the ice cream.

Chapter 4

You know you're in a bad way when even unlimited ice cream can't cheer you up.

I'd gotten up early that morning. In the wintertime in Alaska, it's hard to tell the time because it is always so dark. So when I looked at the clock and saw that it was seven in the morning, I flipped over onto my stomach and tried to stay still. I'd had dreams about skiing with Jake. I was flying down the mountain and had assumed that Jake was right behind me. I kept looking over my shoulder, searching for him. He was too far up the hill for me to see him. I kept shouting, "Catch me! Catch me!" but my voice was lost in the wind.

I woke up just as I was about to crash into Will Parker, who was darting in and out of the trees on his snowboard, with Sabrina Hartley wrapped around his waist. This, as I stretched myself awake, I knew was silly. First of all, you can't double up on a snowboard. And if you could, there's no way Will Parker would let Sabrina Hartley anywhere near his board. Not that he doesn't like her. Will's too easygoing to not like anybody. But he loves his boards more than he loves people, and he probably wouldn't let Scarlett Johansson double up with him.

Anyway, I was awake early, and from the minute I plunked my feet down onto the icy cold of my bedroom floor, I couldn't get the image of Jake throwing snowballs at that girl out of my head. I didn't know what I'd done that he didn't like me anymore, and I obsessed about it through breakfast (which I couldn't eat), through an hour of mindless video-game playing with my brother (he kept killing me over and over; which was fitting, I guess), and through my sad attempts to clean the kitchen for my mom.

Finally I just gave up. I went into Snow Cones early. Normally we don't open until eleven in the morning, but my mother had to come down to do some work in the back office.

I sat in the front and made ice-cream concoctions. I tasted probably twelve different sundaes, and all that did for my heartache was give it a matching stomachache.

The first full winter after I met Jake, I created a milk shake for him. I called it the Jessie Whitman Special Love Shake. It was made with strawberry ice cream, graham crackers, and chopped-up chocolate chips. Right now I was bashing graham crackers into dust, creating a pile of Love Shake ingredients that would never be tasted by another. It reminded me of my heart, how my heart felt crushed.

I looked up and peered out the glass front door of Snow Cones. It was close to eleven and the sun was finally out. Not strong, but at least now you could see the outline of skiers careening down the mountain. The floodlights were on. They'd stay on all day long during this time of winter. People were milling the streets, drinking from large cardboard cups of coffee, lugging skis and snowboards and sleds around. On the horizon you could see the faint outline of some of the mountains from Denali.

This meant the day's weather would be clear and fine. A terrible day to be heartbroken.

A young girl rapped on the glass window, the window that was at the far side of the bar I was standing behind. I gave her the "in five minutes" sign with my hand. She walked to the front door to wait, and I returned to my pile of graham-crackery sadness.

Several things bothered me.

First, I was pretty sure I'd been dumped. Me! I had taken for granted that I had a boyfriend who loved me. It gave me some sense of comfort roaming the cutthroat halls of Willow High. Even if I sometimes felt like an anonymous girl trying to sign people up for clubs that nobody wanted to join and desperately avoiding the callous opinions of Sabrina and her girly, idiot minions, I knew I had someone who thought I was completely special. The thought of having to go back to school, with nothing to look forward to while wasting away playing dodgeball and studying earth samples, made me want to cry.

And now who would I daydream about? I

spent a lot of time in fantasyland, and it would be a lonely place indeed if no boyfriend lived there. What would I spend my time contemplating? Flavors of ice cream? And my future looked bleak too. Jake and I had had plans to travel the country's national park system after I graduated. We'd been talking about this for years, and now what? Something I'd been planning since I was thirteen was just not a possibility anymore? How was that fair? I wanted to go to Yosemite and Yellowstone and Glacier. And I wanted to go to the Southwest, to where there were cacti and desert and sagebrush. Would Jake insert Evie into all the plans *I* had made?

Even worse was, I didn't know why he didn't like me anymore. I hadn't said or done anything differently. I hadn't cheated on him—not that there were any boys in town who I liked enough to cheat on him with. And who *really* cheated on their boyfriends? I mean, other than devious girls like Sabrina. I slammed my fist into the pile of graham crackers, thinking about how mean Sabrina could be to Cam.

She'd cut him down in front of people and then in the very next second be flirty and fun to Will. But she still had a boyfriend, and girls like me and Abby didn't. Maybe I should've been a little meaner to Jake.

I pounded my fist into the graham crackers over and over, grinding them into oblivion. The crackers were being pulverized into a fine dust, and with each downward punch I remembered how sad I had felt waiting by the phone the previous night, just because he had said he would call.

"Jessie." With a fist covered in food, I looked up to see my petite mom in the doorway that led behind the counter to the storage closet, the freezer, and her little office. She held up her arm and pointed to her wrist. "Time, sweetie." Just as she spoke, the little girl who was waiting outside knocked on the door with all the verve that I had used on the poor ingredients.

"Sorry," I said to my mother, brushing my hands off over the sink. "I'm on it." My voice must have sounded thick, because my mother walked toward me and ran a finger through the pile of crumbs I'd created.

"Take it easy on the food, okay?"

I nodded my head quickly, and bit my lip to keep from crying.

My mom narrowed her eyes at me, and said, "I don't believe the world has ended. You'll be just fine." With that she brushed the crumbs into a wastepaper basket and kissed me on the head.

"Yes, ma'am," I said.

"Call me if you need me," my mother said, and then disappeared back into her office.

I walked to the door and opened it, flipping the CLOSED sign over to the OPEN side.

A stream of people poured in, lugging all manner of skis and snowboards in behind them.

"I'll have vanilla with honey sauce, please," the little girl who had been waiting said in a clear voice.

"Make that two," her mother said to me kindly.

I set to work, and by the time I handed the woman two cups full of ice cream, I saw that Abby and Erin were sitting on stools on the other side of the counter, waiting for me.

Once I tended to all the other customers, I pulled out a pair of small dishes and filled them with the girls' favorites. Sweet cream and berries for Abby and black-licorice mint for Erin.

"Ice cream for lunch. Awesome," Erin said before shoving in a huge mouthful.

"Are you going to have any?" Abby asked me.

"No." I looked around the shop, then at each of the tubs sitting in the horizontal cooler. Chocolate, strawberry, vanilla, mint, peanut butter, pistachio, red velvet cake, sweet cream, cookie dough. Nothing looked good. I hoped that being single didn't mean that I'd lost my taste for ice cream!

"How do you feel today?" Erin inquired matter-of-factly.

"Terrible." I plopped my head into my hands and blew the bangs from my forehead with a steady stream of depressed air.

Abby reached across and rubbed my shoulder. "At least you have us."

"Yeah," I sighed. "I'm so depressed, I found

myself wishing that I had homework to do."

Erin's face was one of complete horror. "Homework? What?"

"Well, at least it'd be something to do, so that my mind would be occupied."

"Oh, God, you *are* in a bad way."

"Jess, I'm going to tell you how I got over it when Cam started dating Sabrina."

Erin arched an eyebrow. "You haven't gotten over that yet."

Abby ate a spoonful of ice cream. "Well, Erin, he was my first love, even if he didn't know it. You fall in love and see how it hurts when they abandon you. Oh!" Abby looked at me. Her mouth was in a pitiful expression, an *O* of sorrow.

"God, I've been abandoned." I could barely lift my head from my hands when the little girl came back to the counter to ask for napkins.

Erin finished her black-licorice mint and pushed the empty cup toward me. "So, I did some digging," she said as I refilled her dish.

"Yeah?" I asked.

"Yeah. Mrs. Stewart was at the front desk this morning and she sure was talkative." She slid forward on her stool, and Abby followed suit. I looked around at the customers inside Snow Cones, to make sure nobody could overhear whatever it was that Erin was about to tell me.

"You sure you want to hear?"

"How bad is it?"

"Nothing major, just some basic biographical intel."

"Give it to me." For some reason, the fact that Erin had investigated on my behalf spurred my appetite. As she talked, I spooned some lavender ice cream into a clean dish, taking the last bite from the scooper even though my mother would fire me if she saw me do that.

"Evie Stewart. She's eighteen, from Boise, Idaho."

"We knew that already," Abby said.

"How does he know a girl from Idaho anyway?" I stabbed my spoon into my lavender ice cream.

"Her father went to law school with Jake's dad, and they've been friends, like, forever. They've been planning this joint family trip for years."

"For years?" Abby asked, her voice a squeak. I understood what she was asking. She was asking if that meant that Jake and Evie had been dating. For years.

I continued to take it all out on my lavender ice cream. "That rat-fink jerk bastard." My voice got very, very loud on that last word, and the mother of the young honey vanilla ice-cream eater covered her daughter's ears and gave me a dirty look.

"Sorry, ma'am."

"Language!"

I was terrified that my mother would appear so I quickly scooped two free dishes of ice cream and brought them to her. "I'm really sorry, ma'am," I began to explain. "My boyfriend just dumped me. Have some free ice cream." The woman looked at me like I was handing her cups full of poison. I couldn't say I blamed her. I *felt* unhinged. Lord knows what impression I was making.

Then, the bells attached to the front door rang out, signaling that my horrible day was about to take a dramatic turn for the worse. In walked Sabrina, Hannah, and Stephanie, like three teenage Minions of Doom. There were few things that could make me feel worse than I already did, but having the unfortunate circumstances of my newfound singledom on display certainly was one of them.

My instinct for self-preservation kicked in. "Get out!" I snarled.

Sabrina only laughed, and that's when I heard the footsteps of my mother. I swear the woman has bad-daughter-behavior radar.

"Hello, girls," my mother welcomed them.

"Hello, Mrs. Whitman!" Sabrina spoke the way she did to the principal of our school, like she was honored to be just *talking* to my mother. "We were just shopping in town, and the three of us thought, 'We *can't* go on without a delicious treat from *Snow Cones*.'"

Erin pretended to gag, and Abby put her head down to keep from laughing. My mother walked forward to where Sabrina and her crew stood. "Is that right?" Her voice was dripping with disbelief. "How about some lavender for you then, or our special of the day. It's chocolate with a hint of basil." These were the moments when I felt lucky to have my mother on my side. She was selling them the two most expensive flavors.

"I'll have the lavender, please."

Erin stood on the rung of her stool, picked up my cup of half-eaten lavender ice cream, and tossed it into the trash.

I stood back with my arms crossed while my mother waited on the Minions. I refused to give them any joy, even of the dairy variety. My mother got them their ice cream without another glance, then turned to me as she headed back to her office. "Try not to use words like 'bastard' in front of the customers." She kissed my head and I could feel my face getting hot. I hated when she treated me like a little kid in public, especially in front of girls like Sabrina, who could drive and probably had gone all the way and whose mother lived half the year in a whole other state!

Once my mother left, Sabrina made a big show of choosing a stool to sit on. Stephanie and Hannah flurried to her side, and together, the three of them pretended to eat their ice cream, while making vicious eyes at me the whole time. I tried to ignore them, and stood by Erin and Abby.

Finally Sabrina put her spoon down, and began to talk loudly to her two stupid friends about the Northern Lights Ball. "Mom sent me the prettiest pair of shoes to go with my dress. They're blue satin." She looked at me pointedly. "Jessie, do you have your shoes yet? Or was the seamstress here"—she pointed at Abby— "going to make them for you? Carve them from wood maybe?"

Then Stephanie chimed in, "You don't even have a date anymore, so you won't be able to go, will you?"

Then they burst into laughter. They were still entertaining themselves with conspiratorial laughter when the door opened. At the sight of Will Parker, Sabrina sat taller on her stool. She didn't even try to hide her admiration of him when Cam strolled in after him. What was going on? Why were the coolest kids in school descending on the shop on what was possibly the worst day of my life?

"Hey, Will," Sabrina cooed as Cam walked to where she sat, and put a foot up on the lower rung of her stool. Erin gave him a very dirty look, and he began to blush when he saw Abby.

"Hey, Abby," he said quietly. This caused Sabrina to scoot closer to Cam, even though she quickly returned her gaze to Will, who stood in the middle of the floor looking at Sabrina and her girls before settling onto the stool next to Erin.

"Gimme some of that," he said, taking Erin's spoon and proceeding to eat her ice cream. Abby flashed a quick look at me. Right then and there I decided that if Abby and I couldn't have love in our lives, I was going to make sure that Erin had some, even if I had to kill Sabrina to do it.

Sabrina didn't take too kindly to Will sitting with the enemy. Her lovely face drew itself into a frown, and Stephanie and Hannah grew deathly quiet.

"Will, we were just talking about the

Northern Lights Ball," Sabrina said out loud, placing a hand over Cam's. Will smiled at me easily, and pushed Erin's empty dish in my direction. I filled it with chocolate. My breakup was bad for my mom's bottom line. I was giving ice cream away.

"Yeah?" Will asked.

"Yeah," Sabrina cooed. "You're going to ride in our limo, right?"

Erin snorted, and I couldn't help myself. "There're no *limousines* in Willow Hill, Sabrina." Erin and Abby both smirked, and Sabrina gave me a death stare.

"*You* going?" Will poked Erin in the ribs. Abby's eyes grew wide.

"Please," Erin snorted. "I'd rather ride in a limo with Sabrina." Then she quickly looked back and forth between me and Will. I recognized that look. It was the look she got when she was about to come up with a masterly sinister plan. "But you know what? Were you going?"

"I don't know. No date," he said with a giant, gleaming white smile. Sabrina's spoon clattered onto the floor.

"You should go with Jessie." Erin's voice got very excited.

"What?" I asked. "No, I'm not going now." I stage-whispered this, like my mom does when she doesn't want my brother, Brian, to know that the slopes are still open.

"You have to go with somebody! You can't let Jake just go to the dance with that girl and not be there to stop it! And you can't go without a date."

"She's got a point, you know," Abby chimed in. "And I have the dress all set."

"Will, I don't want to go anymore. So, don't worry."

Will took a bite of ice cream and smiled at me. "Come on, Whitman, don't be chicken. I'll take you. It'll be fun."

"Jessie, you gotta fight fire with fire," Cam chimed in. Sabrina hit him in the arm.

I looked back and forth between Cam and Will. I didn't know what to say. Everything was happening so fast, I couldn't keep up. I was vaguely aware, though, of how Sabrina and the

Minions were staring at me, clearly waiting to hear what I was going to say.

Erin leaned forward and whispered under her breath, "It'll drive Sabrina insane if you go with Will."

I don't know if Will knew that Sabrina liked him, but he heard what Erin said and didn't dispute it. In fact, his grin became even wider, if that was possible. I looked at Abby quickly, hoping she would give me a sign. We both wanted Erin to date somebody, and Will was the only guy she seemed even mildly interested in. Wasn't I sabotaging this possible love match if I went to the Northern Lights Ball with him?

"There's no way you'd want to go to this dance, right, Erin?"

"Please. Not if Johnny Depp were my date."

Abby nodded at me.

"Okay."

"Yeah?" Will asked.

"Yes. It's a date."

Will stood on his stool and high-fived

me. "Yeah, Whitman! One date with me and you'll forget all about that guy anyway." He waggled his eyebrows. Erin shot a triumphant look at Sabrina, who choked on her bite of ice cream.

Chapter 5

"*E*at your peas. Now," my mother commanded me and my brother.

I was having dinner with my family later that night, and I wished I had the power to nod my head and disappear. Mothers have a way of talking about inconsequential things, like eating your vegetables, right when your whole world is falling apart. I mean, peas? Peas? Would peas get me Jake back? I mashed a whole smattering of them with the back of my fork, and then choked them down. Nope. Didn't help. My life was still a heartbreaking episode of a romantic television show.

I sighed and looked around, trying not to yell at my brother even though he was talking about his ice-hockey team as if anyone in the world cared about how many goals he had to score to break the Willow Hill Bantam League record.

At least the house was warm. It was so cold outside, this was the first time I'd felt my toes all day. It was depressing that I was counting being able to feel my toes as a positive thing. I'd sunk so low that I now looked to the fact that I had basic shelter as a silver lining.

In winter, we always ate in our kitchen, a large, pine-paneled room with a wooden island in the middle of it. Next to the table were three floor-to-ceiling glass doors that led out onto a huge deck, a deck my father said was the only reason he agreed to build the house in the first place. In summer, we ate outside around a pine table that was also made by my dad. In the dead of winter, like now, when there was barely any sunlight, we'd sit inside and I'd pass most of our family dinners staring outside at the pine trees and trying to make out the shapes of the mountain in the background.

There was a baby deer and her momma in our yard just now, grazing. That was a positive, yes? God. I was going to start counting the fact that I was breathing as a good thing.

"Look! A deer!" Brian exclaimed, and pointed at the window. When my father and mother turned to look, Brian snuck a handful of peas into the mouth of our shaggy brown dog, Bear. I pushed my food around my plate absentmindedly.

"Jessie. The food goes in your mouth," my father pronounced. I looked up to find that he was looking at me. "You're a growing girl. Eat."

My father is a typical Alaskan. He's huge, like, six five and burly. He's got a beard that used to be really shaggy until my mother made him start trimming it. He always wears flannel and denim and baseball caps. And he's real outdoorsy. He loves to fish and fly his plane and hike and build things. And he hates it when I'm depressed. He says that he can't handle sad girls in his house.

"She'll eat when she's hungry, Bart," my mother said. "Eat," she commanded me.

Brian assumed that my parents were too concerned with my eating habits to notice if he fed another handful of peas to the dog.

"Hey!" I pointed at him on purpose to rat him out. He threw his arms up in anger.

"Brian! Go wash your hands, right now!"

My brother did what my mother said. While he was in the kitchen, noisily sloshing water around the sink and making bombing noises—he was pretending that the soap dispenser was an airplane and his hands were the target—my mother turned her laserlike gaze on me.

"Jessie is going to the Northern Lights dance with Will Parker," she said, staring at me but talking to my father.

"Mom!" I shouted at her. I wasn't surprised that she knew this. I hadn't told her, but my mother was omniscient. She knew everything.

My dad stared at me. "Really? What about the pretty kid from the States?"

I threw my fork down with a clatter. "Dad," my voice sounded really whiny, even to me, "Jake's not *pretty* and he's from Alaska."

My dad widened his eyes in annoyed disagreement. He didn't consider Juneau to be part of Alaska, because it was so close to the mainland and because he claimed all the people who lived down there were soft and couldn't hack it in the wilds of the north.

"Bart," my mother said in a singsong voice. When my father looked at her, she drew a finger across her neck a few times, to signal to him to let it drop. Even though she was the one who brought it up.

"Mom, I can see you."

"Well, I'm just saying we don't have to talk about this."

"There are no secrets at this table," my father said as he popped a large piece of steak in his mouth. Just then a large thudding sound came from the kitchen sink, punctuated by my brother's screeching yell.

"Brian! Clean that up!" My mother shouted, before she could even see what he'd done. She got up to inspect the damage in the kitchen.

"Think he broke anything?" my father asked me.

"Hopefully his face," I pouted, still pushing peas around my plate.

"Tell me."

I sighed and looked at my dad without lifting my head from my hand. "It's nothing."

My father looked at me and didn't say anything.

"Just that Jake is going to the dance with another girl," I mumbled.

He again didn't say anything and looked anxiously toward my mother, who was still in the kitchen. He talked a good game about no secrets, but heart-to-hearts with me made him nervous. "Annie!"

"Give me two seconds, Bart."

I started laughing. "Dad, you can handle a bear, but you can't handle talking to your own daughter?"

He swallowed and wiped his mouth with a napkin. "Okay." He folded his hands and placed them in his lap and turned toward me.

"Yeah? You want to give this a crack?"

My father nodded. "You don't scare me."

"Okay," I said, smiling for the first time since I'd been home. "Let's say you wanted a new, um, *airplane*."

My father looked at me like one of us was an idiot. "A new *airplane*." He nodded, understanding that I wasn't talking about airplanes.

"Right. You want a new airplane. Before you got that new airplane, wouldn't you tell the old airplane that you were getting a new airplane?"

"Would I tell the old airplane?"

"You know what I mean!"

My father took a deep breath and looked into the kitchen. I could tell he was desperate for my mother to return. "Um, I don't talk to my airplanes."

"Dad. First of all, I've heard you talk to your airplanes." This was true. He tended to babytalk them while he flew. "But that's not what I'm talking about."

Now he began slicing his steak into large pieces that were only bite-sized to a man as big as my dad. "Can you just tell me what we're talking about?"

I sighed. I didn't want to have to admit to my dad that I might have been dumped. "Forget it."

My father again looked nervously to the kitchen. "Um. You go to the dance with Will Parker. He's a good kid. Forget that other softy."

I just looked at him. He widened his eyes and grinned, then patted me on the cheek. "Don't tell me your old dad can't handle your problems."

After dinner I was lying on my bed, listening to a depressing playlist of songs that Erin had emailed. She'd said that they would make me feel better, but so far they were making me feel sadder. The sound of the female singer wailing into the microphone, in fact, made me want to do myself serious harm.

Normally my bedroom was a cozy sanctuary. Our house was a three-floor cabin, and my room was on the very top floor. The ceiling sloped down on one side and met the wall at about five and a half feet. This was where Dad built me a desk and a matching bookcase. Most of the walls were made of wood, but there was one wall painted peach, and I had hung jewelry and posters and pictures of several national parks on it. I had a rocking chair and a beanbag chair and a big queen-sized bed. It was a room to be proud of. Erin's room was half this big, and Abby had to share with her little sister. This was why they spent most of their free time here, unless we were at Snow Cones pigging out on ice cream or at the resort trying to stay out of Mean Agnes's line of vision.

Right now I felt anything but cozy. I rolled over onto my stomach and reached for my laptop, which was on the floor. I hit the MUTE button quickly to stop the caterwaul of despair, and then picked up the computer, rolled back over, and balanced it on my lap.

Breathing deeply, I opened up my Jake file. There were pictures of our trip to Denali, pictures of our many ski adventures, pictures of us riding on the back of Mr. Winter's dogsled. My favorite, which I'd printed out and put in a frame on my nightstand, was of the two of us standing at the top of Mount Crow. We'd spent the day hiking around, and just as the sun began to set, he'd asked a passerby to take our picture. Behind our smiling, laughing faces was a sky full of bright orange and pink prettiness. Jake's arm was around me and his head was bent toward mine so that the tips of our hats were touching.

I don't know what possessed me, but I suddenly leaped from my bed. My laptop fell crashing to the floor. I ran to my closet and flung the door open, surveying the clothes within. There were racks of flannel shirts and thick wool sweaters beside corduroy pants in every color imaginable. I thought about Sabrina and what her closet probably looked like. There was likely no *flannel* in it. I bet Evie didn't even own flannel.

Well, I couldn't transform myself into a fashion icon. There was no time. I pulled down a soft baby blue cashmere sweater my father had bought me in Seattle, and then searched for the newest, darkest, cleanest jeans I could find. Then I went to my mom's closet and searched for the pair of black boots that she told me I could never wear because they were unseemly for a teenage girl. I shoved the boots into a backpack, hoping that they would retain their shape. I brushed my hair until it shone, and then plugged in my curling iron and worked on it until there were wavy pieces framing my face. I put on lip gloss and some mascara and a pair of earrings I never wore because they pulled on my ears and kind of hurt.

Stepping back, I surveyed myself in the antique, full-length mirror that sat in a wooden stand my father made, and took a breath. I actually looked pretty good, and that was without the boots.

I reached for a scarf and wrapped it around my neck. I'd be forgoing a coat; I didn't have one that didn't make me look like I was nine years old or a truck driver from the Arctic Circle.

It wasn't until I'd jumped from my window onto the roof, and then landed in the backyard with only Bear seeing me, that I really committed to sneaking out of my house. And it wasn't until I was walking along the path from my house to the main road that led into town that I decided where I was going.

Staring at those pictures, the ones of me and Jake, I realized that I deserved more than this. I deserved a conversation at least. That's what my mother would have demanded. If my dad suddenly showed up at our house with another woman, she'd demand answers!

I shoved my hands in my pockets and raised my shoulders to brace against the wind, laughing at the idea of my dad ever doing that. First of all, he was my dad, but also, he was terrified of my mother. He'd never do *anything* that would upset her.

I kept walking. The boots were pinching my toes, and as it had started snowing slightly, I was having a hard time getting any traction. I thought longingly of my real boots, which were currently in my backpack, hidden in the bushes by the turnoff to Old Man Jones's yurt. I also thought longingly of my coat, which was in my closet doing me no good. In my room, planning to brave the elements for style seemed like a good idea. Out here, where it was windy and snowy and there was hardly any moonlight, it didn't seem so smart.

But what could I do? I wanted answers and I deserved them. So what if it was almost ten o'clock at night? So what if I was going to get frostbite and likely lose a couple of fingers? So what? What was all this in the face of lost love?

When I got to the main street in town, I veered to the left, and cut across the parking lot of the Mountain Diner. This was the quickest route to the edge of the resort where the cabins were, but as soon as I stepped into the lamp-lit lot, I realized what a mistake it was to come this way. Will, Jay, and Cam were huddled around the back of Jay's pickup truck, loading in their skis and snowboards. Sabrina lounged against the back bumper and from all the way on the other side of the lot, I could tell that she was whining at Cam. I took a deep breath and tried to hide in the shadows. It wasn't that I was afraid of them, but I really didn't feel like hearing about it from Sabrina.

But after two steps I was overtaken by a sneezing fit. It had been a matter of time. My nose had been getting progressively runnier as

I walked, but God hated me sometimes and that's why I started sneezing in front of everybody.

Will, whose back had been to me, turned to find the source of the noise. Sabrina pointed in my direction and laughed as Stephanie and Hannah huddled around her and began whispering furiously in her ears.

"Is that my date?" Will called across the lot. I wanted to drop dead of embarrassment. But instead of fleeing the scene, I waved my hand in the air, and said, "Hey," before continuing on.

"Whitman!" Will pushed his board into the truck and came running for me. I had no choice but to stop.

"What's up?" I asked him.

As he approached me, I could see his expression turn from relaxation to mild confusion. "Where's your coat?"

"Um, uh. Home," I responded lamely.

"You visiting Erin? She's still behind the desk. Mean Agnes caught her throwing away the beef jerky from the gift shop, so she's working extra to cover the cost. Like resort detention."

I looked toward the resort and then back at Will, trying to decide whether or not to admit what I was up to. But lying was too much trouble, so I faced him, wrapping my arms around me to keep warm. "Hey, have you seen Jake around tonight?"

"Ah," he said, getting it. "Nope, not on the slopes anyway, and he wasn't in there." He gestured to the diner. Sabrina and the Minions eyed me suspiciously from over by Will's truck.

"Oh, okay. Well, cool. I'll see you, Will, and listen, thanks for, you know, the ball, and everything. If you change your mind, it's no big deal."

Will cocked his head. "No way are you weaseling out of this. The town deserves to see me in a tux." Then he looked over his shoulder and stepped closer to me. "Jessie—"

"Yeah?"

"Take my coat, okay?"

"Huh? I don't need it."

"Jessie." He gave me a "let's be real" look. "You're shivering. And it's a long way to those cabins. Just take it." He removed his coat, the white puffy parka with the large X over the right side, and put it around my shoulders. Then he walked back to the truck.

I was so pleased at the mortified look on Sabrina's face that it took me a few seconds to realize that Will had known where I was heading.

By the time I reached the cabins, it was well after ten thirty and I was a Popsicle, even in Will's heavy coat. I walked to the Reids' front door, but it was late and Jake's mom was kind of strict. So instead of ringing the doorbell, I clambered across the porch that wrapped around the entire house, and stood on the railing. Jake's window loomed up above me. There was a light on and music coming from his room, so I knew that he was there. Also, it seemed to be hard rock, so that gave me confidence that Evie wasn't with him. Not that Mrs. Reid would let him have a girl in his room. Although, maybe that was just me. Maybe she let girls from Boise do whatever they wanted.

Clinging to the side of the house with one

hand, I stood on my tiptoes and reached for his window. No good. I'm short like my mom, and didn't even come close.

I flattened my feet and remained on the railing, thinking about my next move. Finally, I cupped my hands around my mouth and whisper-yelled, "Jake! Jake!" But it was windy and the falling snow had picked up, which caused a howling sound, so there was no way he could hear me.

I took a deep breath and looked around his backyard. The swing set sat silently, stilly in the yard, lit up by a slice of moonlight that was half covered by clouds. There was a stand of trees that divided this cabin from the one next door. I leaped off the railing and landed awkwardly, slipping back and forth before I could get any balance. These boots weren't made for these kinds of covert ops. I gritted my teeth against the pain, and limped over to the trees. The ground was mostly covered with snow, but a decent-sized branch poked up from the white, and I grabbed it and pulled it with both hands until it came loose.

Armed with my weapon, I re-climbed the railing and raised the branch. Yes! It reached the window. I tapped with all my might, only to worry that I'd broken the window.

And suddenly he was there. Jake was at the window looking down into the yard. He looked toasty warm, in a long-sleeved red shirt. His hair was floppy in an extra-cute way. I waved wildly so that he'd see me, and almost lost my balance. He did a double take, then put a finger up to the window to signal that I should wait before disappearing back into his room.

After a minute, he reappeared in the window, wearing a thick sweater. He opened the window wide, and then removed the winter screen. "Jessie! You're gonna get me in trouble."

I didn't say anything. I didn't have to, he was already climbing out of the window. I felt a little thrill that he was breaking the rules just to see me.

"Is anybody in there?" He pointed downward, and I peered into the first floor windows, which were dark.

"No, no, you're clear."

"Well, move!" He needed the railing to stop

himself from dropping two stories onto the porch. I climbed down as fast as I could, but my ankle felt a little gimpy from my earlier fall.

Jake's feet landed squarely on the railing, as if he'd climbed out of his window every night. It struck me that we could've been meeting secretly like this the whole time we knew each other, but I didn't think it was the time or place to mention that.

Once he was standing in front of me on the porch, I could see that he was really annoyed, and the excitement I felt turned to dread. I suddenly was overwhelmed with the same kind of feelings as when I first met him, that he was far too cute a guy to be talking to me.

"You're going to get me in so much trouble." He grabbed my arm and led me from the porch to the swings. He sat on one and stared at me. "What are you doing here?"

"Won't your parents see?" I pointed to the kitchen windows—they were wall-sized. I could see plainly into the house. Mr. and Mrs. Reid were drinking glasses of wine and reading to each other from the paper.

"Jessie, just tell me why you're here."

I swallowed hard. There was something about Jake that had always been different than all the other boys I knew. He was more *mature*, I guess. He had more in his head than snow. Erin could call him wishy-washy all she wanted, but in moments like these, he was very straightforward.

"Well?"

I pulled Will's coat closer around me to keep out the chill and to buy time. I'd come all the way out here, and now that I'd gotten him face-to-face, I didn't know what I wanted to say.

"Jessie!"

"How come you didn't call me?" I spat out.

This seemed to disarm him. He looked to the ground and began pushing himself back and forth on the swing. "I'm sorry," he muttered to the ground.

"If you wanted to break up," I had a hard time getting that phrase out, "you should've just told me."

"I know." He kept looking at the ground.

"It's not nice to stop talking to somebody!"

"Keep your voice down, geez!"

I was good and sad now. It had been a matter of time before he realized that I was just a girl from a tourist town, really. "So . . . what, you just don't like me anymore?"

"No! No, I like you. I just, I don't know."

"You don't know?" His no-answer answers were causing me serious pain. I wasn't sure what his problem was. "I'm giving you the chance to just tell me what I did wrong. So could you please just get on with it?"

He looked at me then and took a deep breath. "Jessie, you didn't do anything wrong."

"No?" I was shivering by this point. My teeth were chattering and I could only imagine how red my nose was.

"No." He stood up from the swing then and said, "I can't just hang out here, my parents are going to see me." Then he reached for me and pulled my coat tight around me. "And you're going to catch a cold."

He didn't let go of my coat. In fact, he started tracing the big embroidered X with his fingers. And he was standing kind of close to me. I was getting confused. He raised his eyes and smiled a sad smile at me. Then we both heard his mother call, "Jake? Jake?" from inside the house.

"Oh man. I gotta go. I'll talk to you later, okay?" Then, looking quickly into the house to make sure nobody was looking, he kissed me lightly on the lips before scampering back to the railing and pulling himself into his window.

Chapter 6

"*So* what do you think that means?" I was leaning against a desk that was piled high with papers and pencils and ski passes and old reservation books.

"It means he's wishy-washy. Like I always said," Erin replied, barely looking at me. She was trying unsuccessfully to cram a stack of papers into a drawer that was already overflowing. "God, I hate that woman!" she shouted in frustration. Erin was spending her Friday morning filing Agnes's various papers and cleaning her office, her punishment for stealing the reservation book.

"How did she find out about the book anyway?" I asked idly.

"You could help me, you know," Erin said with narrowed black-rimmed eyes. "If you're hanging out here, you should file." She tapped a pile of papers by her, which caused them to tumble onto the floor in disarray. "Argh!"

"Relax, relax, I'll help." I bent down and began sorting through the pile that had just fallen. "So, can we get back to Jake and the fact that he kissed me?"

Erin stopped what she was doing. "You know what I think? I think it meant nothing. I think Jake will kiss whoever's in front of him."

"I'm not helping anymore." I kicked the pile that I had just straightened so the papers fell into Erin's lap.

"Mature," she said.

I was pouting, I knew it. But Erin had a way of summing up a situation in ways that you didn't always want to hear, and this wasn't one of the times I was looking for bracing reality. "How about a little optimism?" I muttered.

"Fine, you want optimism? Maybe Jake realized, while looking at you late at night, hair askew, nose running, desperately having stalked him, that he'd made a big mistake. Better?"

"My hair wasn't askew." There was nothing

else to say, so I began helping her organize all the junk.

Erin stopped what she was doing. "Why don't you just ask him what it meant?"

"I will, I will. I just, I don't know. Maybe I don't want the answer."

Erin looked at me and shook her head. "This is why I refuse to fall in love."

"Are you sure you want to do this?" Abby was pulling at the collar of her ski jacket. "God, this thing is choking me!" Abby wasn't what you'd call a skier. In fact, she wasn't altogether coordinated, so she didn't go in much for outdoor sports. She wore the clothes, though, although this jacket seemed to be giving her trouble.

"You can go if you want to. I'm staying right here until he shows up." We were in one of the lodges. This one was a square-shaped room near the bottom of the two black-diamond hills. It was early in the afternoon, and the room was packed with people who were taking a lunch break from the slopes. There was a counter along the far back wall where you could order waters or hot chocolates or snacks, like pretzels and hot dogs. But even with all that food, the lodge smelled like cinnamon and vanilla and burning birch logs. There was always a fire burning right in the center of the room. It was a cozy spot, actually, with the centerpiece fireplace and the warm couches and benches that were situated around it.

This is where Abby and I were camped out. I had a cup of hot chocolate that I was hardly touching, and Abby was finishing off a bottle of cranberry iced tea. We were waiting.

After Erin finished cleaning the papers out of Agnes's office, she pulled the lists of purchased ski passes. It turned out that Evie hadn't bought a ski pass, but Jake and his family definitely had. Erin then pulled the spa logs and we saw that Evie would be spending much of her time at Mount Crow getting manicures and massages.

I devised a plan: I would lie in wait for the Reids to arrive at the lodge, and then I could "run into" Jake. I had purposely not called him today, because I didn't want him to think that I was freaking out about one little kiss, even though I clearly *was* freaking out about it. But if we "ran into" each other, then he'd have to acknowledge me, and then I could maybe figure out whether that kiss had meant that our love was rekindled or if that was his new standard way of saying good-bye to people. I was hoping for the former.

Because one thing I knew: I was never going to do better than Jake Reid. Just seeing him for that brief moment in his yard, I was surer than ever. We both loved to ski. We both wanted to travel. I was the only one who knew about the birthmark on his back, the one shaped like a seagull. Surely he wouldn't show Evie that. And he was the only one I could tell my dreams to, about going to UAA and then moving to the Lower States and never having to wear a pair of thermal underwear under my jeans again.

"Oh! We're on!" I exclaimed suddenly as Mrs. Reid walked through the entrance to the lodge, followed by Jake and an energetic firecracker named Madison, his little sister. Before I even had a chance to tell Abby what the plan was (which I hadn't done before because, as usual, I hadn't come up with a plan yet) Madison screamed at the top of her lungs, "Jessie!"

Madison's and Jake's mother turned to look at what her daughter was screeching at, and I waved wildly.

As Madison flew toward me in a whirlwind of brown braids, I caught Jake's expression. He looked grumpy and annoyed, just as he had when he saw me at his window. This was check one in the "that kiss didn't mean anything" column.

"Jessie! I'm so glad to see you!" Madison leaped into the air, and I stood up and caught her, swinging her around.

"You're so big!" I screamed, and hugged her close.

"I know! I'm the biggest girl in the second grade," she said very proudly. Her face looked like a rounder, frecklier version of Jake's, but with a girl's smile, a turned-up nose, and long eyelashes that your average supermodel would kill for.

"You're doing the black-diamond hills this

year, Mad?" I asked, setting her down.

"That's right, we promised, as long as one of us is with her at all times. How are you, Jessie?" Mrs. Reid was standing there, trying to smooth down Madison's hair, which was sticking out in all directions.

"I'm good, Mrs. Reid."

She smiled at me and I stole a quick glance at Jake, to show him that his family still loved me.

"Madison, let's go!" Jake snapped at her from across the lodge.

"Shut up, Jake, I'm allowed to talk to her. Just because you broke up with her, doesn't mean we're not friends anymore, right, Jessie?"

I felt like I'd been slapped in the face. *You broke up with her.* For a moment I thought I was going to cry, but I ground my teeth and answered the little girl as sure-voiced as I could, "That's right, Mad."

Mrs. Reid looked at me sadly, which made me feel even more terrible, and pulled Madison away from me. "Let's go, sweetheart, we want to get as many runs in as we can."

"Okay, Mom," and Madison ran out the door. She had a lot of energy.

"It's nice to see you, Jessie," Mrs. Reid said to me. "You look good." She smiled quickly, then followed her daughter out to the slopes.

I watched them go, and then Abby rose from her spot on the couch and nudged my arm. When she got my attention, she pointed at the hot-dog counter so that I could see that Jake hadn't followed them outside. "Why don't I go find Erin and see if Mean Agnes will let her take a break?"

I still felt like breaking into sobs from what Madison had said. "I don't think—" Abby touched my arm again. "But what should I say?" I asked, trying to gather my courage.

Abby blew out a breath. "I don't know, Jessie. Obviously I know nothing about getting the guy you want." And then she was gone. She barely nodded to Jake on the way out of the lodge.

Jake saw that I was standing in the middle of the room. He stayed where he was. He was in his bright red coat and goggles and had a pair of shiny new ski boots dangling in his hand.

Well, I couldn't very well just stand there and gawk at him, my patheticness on display for the whole lodge to see. And really, I had designed this whole run-in, so what was my problem? I swallowed hard, trying to forget the phrase "You broke up with her."

I walked up to him and said with all the coolness I could muster, "Hey."

"Hey," he responded. He kept about a foot and a half distance between us and I couldn't decide what that meant.

"First run of the season?" I asked, trying very hard to sound casual even though I could still feel the blood rushing to my feet.

"Yeah. You going today?"

"Nah," I responded truthfully. "I think I kind of hurt my ankle, jumping off your porch."

He clasped his hands behind his back, and this I took as a really bad sign. He was uncomfortable in my presence. Maybe because he thought we were broken up. But maybe it was because he really wanted to kiss me again.

"Were you waiting here for me, then?"

This threw me for a loop. It was one thing to be caught stalking. It was quite another to admit it. "No!"

He snorted. "Then what are you doing here?"

"I believe that I'm allowed to be anywhere I want. It's my town, actually."

His eyes narrowed, and part of my brain, the Abby part, I guess, whispered to me that this wasn't like us. We'd never been snotty to each other before.

"Whatever."

At that moment, Will burst through the slope entryway in a burst of cold air and windy breeze. He stood in the doorway and peeled off his goggles and hat and then shook his hair out with all his might, like a shaggy, ski-loving dog. The blond girl behind the snack counter called out to him sweetly and tossed him a bottle of water. He grinned at her and drank the whole bottle in one gulp before making a basketball shot with it into the nearby trash can. The girl behind the counter looked like she was going to explode, her smile was so big.

"Whitman!" Will shouted when he saw me. "You gotta get out there!" He pointed gleefully. "There's six feet of powder! Let's you and me go." Then he bounded up to us, nodded at Jake, and tugged on the hem of the green parka that I was wearing. "Where's my coat, lady? It looks way better on you than this green thing."

I was initially embarrassed by Will's putting my coat down, but then I saw that Jake was looking from Will to me to Will again with a confused, shocked look on his face. And I realized in that second that Jake thought that I'd been waiting in the lodge for *Will*, not for him.

I didn't say anything right away, then my nerve found me and I turned to Will and grabbed his hand. "I just wanted to tell you that, um, Abby needs to get your measurements for the dance." This was technically not a lie. In fact, the best part was that this was absolutely true! And at any rate it served Jake right for telling his family that he had broken up with me.

There was a devilish expression on Will's

face and I *knew* that he knew what I was doing. He squeezed my hand and pulled me into him a little bit, and suddenly my heart sped up. "Sure thing. I'll be over later, okay, babe?" Will had a tendency to call all girls "babe" but Jake didn't know that.

The only thing that could have made me happier about this was if Sabrina had been there. I couldn't keep from smiling a little too broadly at Will. "'Kay. See you later, then." He squeezed my hand again and then headed back out to the slopes, but gave me a wink when he was out of Jake's line of sight.

Once he was gone, I turned back to Jake and that's when the thrill of our little game left me and I was suddenly unsure of what I had hoped to accomplish by being in the lodge in the first place. Everything was getting away from me. Now not only did I *not* know whether Jake had meant anything by kissing me, but now I'd probably gone and planted a seed of doubt in his mind about whether or not I'd even wanted to be kissed in the first place.

"Jake—"

But I couldn't finish whatever it was that I was going to say, because Jake spun on his heel and followed Will's path out to the slopes, without so much as a backward look at me.

Chapter 7

"Just because you broke up with her, doesn't mean we're not friends anymore, right, Jessie?"

I was facing a full-length reflection of me in Abby's ball gown, but all I could see in my bedroom mirror was little Madison Reid repeating, over and over, the phrase: *You broke up with her.*

"Jessie! Hello?" I felt a sharp jab in my ribs.

"Huh?" I turned to see Erin and Abby staring at me.

"Don't keep Abby in suspense. Look at her. She's about to faint."

Erin was right. Abby was pale from holding her breath. She thought I hated the dress!

"Oh, Abby, I'm sorry." I turned back to the mirror and took in the sight.

I looked like a real, live fairy-tale princess.

If you excluded the sadness in my eyes and the pasty white Alaskan skin tone, then I was prettier than I'd ever been, even if I seemed to be trapped in a prison of white, gauzy netting.

"So?" Abby's nervous face appeared behind mine in the mirror. You couldn't see her body, though, because of all the lace.

"*I* think you look like you got eaten by a fabric monster," Erin said matter-of-factly from the rocking chair in the corner of my room. On her lap was the thickest book I'd ever seen anyone attempt to read.

"Erin!" I said, trying to cut off her bluntness. "I like it. It's really, um—"

"Lacy," Erin stated.

Abby's feelings didn't seem to be hurt. Rather, she seemed to take our comments in stride. She walked around the whole of me, which wasn't easy. I seemed to be two yards wide, five feet of which was lace. "I guess I went overboard with the skirt." She giggled softly as she scooped up layers of the white fabric in her hand. "I couldn't help it. It's so soft and pretty!" She threw the fistfuls of fabric up, and the layers settled back down around my legs like newly fallen snow.

"Don't worry, Jess," she said. "I'll fix it. But you like the shape and the fabric and everything?"

I did. I looked like I belonged in a Disney cartoon. The dress had two-inch-wide strappy sleeves and a tight-fitting bodice that Abby was going to decorate with sparkly sequins. And then the skirt, once it was trimmed a little, would cascade around me. It was exactly what we had envisioned: a dress to make a girl cry. When I walked into the dance wearing this, Sabrina would have absolutely no shot at winning the contest no matter what she showed up in.

"You do look pretty, Jess," Erin said. "Even if I need sunglasses to look at you."

Abby shook her head and pointed at Erin. "You're next. I'm making you something white and girly."

Erin snorted. "You'll have to chain me down to get me to wear it."

In days gone by, I'd crack a joke about getting Will Parker to chain Erin down. But something kept me from it. I didn't think it was appropriate now in light of the fact that he was taking me to the dance, and by all appearances, helping me to make Jake jealous. Not that a boy who'd broken up with you could *be* jealous. I shook my head to clear that thought and peered at myself in the mirror again. "Are we done now?" I asked Abby sadly.

"Yeah, you can take it off."

She unzipped the back of the dress and helped me out of it. I put on my real clothes and then flung myself onto my bed, scooting over to where my headboard met the wall. Stretching my legs out in front of me, I reached for the teddy bear that I'd had since I was three. My father had brought it back for me after one of his flights, and even though I was getting too old for such things, Teddy made me feel calmer when things seemed hard to figure. I was lucky that I had two such good friends who didn't think I was a baby for having a stuffed animal. If Sabrina ever knew about it, there'd be no end to my torment.

There was a knock on the door. I shouted,

"Go away," thinking it was Brian. The door opened anyway.

"You've got company, Jessie," my mother said, holding a tray with four steaming mugs on it. As Abby and Erin looked at me with expressions of joy, I stashed Teddy under my covers fast as lightning, even though Jake had seen Teddy many times. Perhaps it was these babyish trappings that were giving him second thoughts about me. "I brought some hot chocolate for you."

"Thanks, Mrs. W," Will Parker said as he barged in, taking a cup from the tray without missing a step. My heart dropped into my feet. Will Parker, the king of Willow High, was in *my* bedroom. Will Parker!

"Erin? Abby?" my mother called to them, and the girls ran for the hot drinks.

"Will, hey," I said, making my voice sound as normal as I could. My mother handed me my own cup. She gave me the "no boys are supposed to be in your room" look. Erin picked up on it right away.

"Mrs. Whitman, did you see the dress that Jessie is wearing to the Northern Lights Ball?"

Abby held it up for my mother to see. Will did a double take as he took in the sight of all the skirt.

"She's fixing it," I said a little too loudly.

"Very pretty, Abby, you have a real gift," my mother said.

"Thanks, Mrs. Whitman. Will's here so I can get his measurements for his tuxedo."

My mother turned to me. "Okay, well, I'm *right downstairs* if you need anything."

Will piped up, "This is delicious hot chocolate, ma'am."

My mother looked at him evenly, muttered, "Um-hmm," and then squinted at me before walking out of the room, quite deliberately leaving the door open.

I shook my head. "Great. Ten bucks says my brother is being paid right now to spy on us."

Will walked to where Abby was sitting, holding a tape measure. "No worries. He's a good kid."

I hated when people who didn't have little brothers referred to Brian as a "good kid." He wasn't a good kid. He was a rambunctious filth machine, who I didn't let into my room.

I stretched out on my bed and sipped my hot chocolate. I'd wager that about thirty girls in my school would have given their skis to have Will Parker in their house. And here he was in my room, standing in front of my mirror, letting Abby wrap his arms and legs in a tape measure. I had to admit, it *was* a little thrilling. I wished we could record this moment and email it to Sabrina.

Abby must have been as awed by Will's presence as I was, because she caught Erin's and my eyes behind Will's back and dropped her jaw wide in shock that Will was there and cooperating.

Erin shook her head. I closed my eyes and leaned my head against the wall.

"The tux won't look like that, will it?" He gestured toward the heap of taffeta and netting lying on the floor.

Erin said, "God, I hope not."

"You don't have to do this if you don't want to."

Three pairs of eyes turned on me.

"What? I'm just saying."

"He's going, and I don't want to hear about

it again," Erin said, finally lifting the book from her lap and moving over to where the two of them stood in front of the mirror.

Will caught my eye and winked. "No worries. I like giving Abby a reason to put her hands all over me." Abby turned bright red. "Did you tell 'em how good an actor I am?"

Will stared at me in the mirror and I lowered my head. I think I was blushing. "No, I didn't."

"Erin, sign me up for an Oscar. We made that Jake kid totally jealous in the lodge, right, Whitman?"

"Er, right." I wanted to sink into my covers. Erin stared at me as if I had six heads.

"Really," she said, contemplating. "How interesting."

"So you didn't, um, *talk*?" Abby asked me, while wrapping some of the taffeta around Will's legs.

"Um, *no*. We didn't."

Erin cleared her throat and asked Will, "Have you ever accidentally kissed a girl?"

I officially wanted to die.

Will caught Erin's eye in the mirror and

answered with a raised eyebrow, "Accidentally? No." He held out his arms so that Abby could measure them. "Have you girls been having kissing 'accidents'?"

Abby said, "Jessie might have."

Will feigned a look of hurt and clutched at his heart. "You're going out with me and kissing other guys?" I threw a pillow at him. Abby was shocked at my boldness and I have to admit that I was too. Will had a way of bringing things out in people, things that they didn't know they had in them.

He caught the pillow with ease, and then, without a trace of a smile or a hint of laughter in his voice, said, "Jessie, if I kissed you it wouldn't be by accident. Trust me."

I don't know if he meant to phrase it that way, but I had never felt so red-faced in my whole life—maybe because he'd used my first name. Abby dropped the tape measure. Erin smirked like an idiot.

I took a deep breath and told myself to get a grip. He was talking about boys in general, and in that respect, I really wanted to believe him. But if that were true, if Jake had kissed me on purpose, because he wanted to, then why had he been so cold to me in the ski lodge? Why'd his family think he'd broken up with me? Did you just go around kissing girls you were broken up with?

I thought for a moment about asking Will this question, but decided not to. Abby was holding my dress up for him and he was telling her that my skirt looked like he could ski down it.

Chapter 8

I had awoken the next morning with every intention of confronting Jake about what Madison had said and about the accidental kiss. But for the next three days, I couldn't get him alone. Every time I "ran into" him on the mountain, he was with Madison or one of Evie's blond sisters, and pretended that he didn't have time to talk to me. During the times he wasn't skiing, Abby and I would linger in the lobby with Erin, but between Erin's grumpy moods and Mean Agnes chasing us out of there, we didn't have much luck. The only time I saw him inside, he ran into the gift shop to avoid me.

When I wasn't at the resort, I'd taken to hiking along the trail in the woods behind the cabins. I normally walked this route even when Jake wasn't in town, because the track wound through a gorgeous section of woods. You could hear the birds sing and see ice glistening on the branches. But now that I was hoping for "run-ins," I made these walks because the trail passed his house. I must have walked by the Reid cabin ten times, and only once did Jake magically appear. He stood on their porch, drinking what was probably a cup of coffee. He was bundled up in baggy ski pants and a huge, fur-lined jacket; it was these kinds of clothes that made my father think he was soft. I called his name. He put his hand in the air, not a wave really but definitely an acknowledgment that I was there, and then hightailed it back into his cabin.

The only time he didn't run when he saw me was when he came into Snow Cones. Evie, it turned out, liked herself some ice cream. The first time the two of them came into the shop, I couldn't believe it. I mean, I would think that *my* family's shop would be off-limits for *their* daytime rendezvous, but apparently Evie's desire for sweets trumped his desire for avoidance. Each time, she'd order vanilla peppermint and he'd have strawberry. The first visit,

I put whipped cream on his in the shape of a heart. He shook his head at me, and I raised my shoulders as if to say, "Whoops!" After that he specifically ordered his with *no* whipped cream.

After three days of this, I decided that I'd had enough. I couldn't keep living like this, hoping that his kiss had meant something but knowing by all the evidence, especially the "you broke up with her" comment, that it probably hadn't. The problem was that while I had even a shred of hope, I had *hope*.

On the fourth day, I was determined to cut work and find Jake, and if I couldn't, then I'd have to show up outside his window again that night.

Unfortunately my mother didn't seem too thrilled with my plan of ditching work. It was either Snow Cones or babysitting. I chose babysitting, something normally on the bottom of the list of things I'd agree to do for my parents. But Brian was desperate to visit Mr. Winter's new litter of puppies, and if we had anything in common, it was our love of animals. I wanted to see them too.

And honestly I needed a break from Snow Cones. I was eating too much ice cream and I needed to fit into Abby's dress. Also, I couldn't take any more Evie sightings.

"Hey, kids!" Mr. Winter called out to me and Brian as we walked around the side of his barn to the pen at the back. He was a big bear of a man, not quite as huge as my dad but big enough that you knew he was born here. He wore overalls with suspenders over a thermal undershirt. He had a red plaid cap on his head and was bending at the waist, petting six small yipping bundles of fur.

Brian broke out into a run and hopped over the pen fence in one fluid motion.

"Easy, big guy!"

"Can I hold 'em? Please? Please? Please?"

Mr. Winter handed him a red-coated little furball and said, "Be gentle now, they're babies yet." Then he walked to the pen door and opened it wide for me.

"Hi, Mr. Winter," I said, walking to where Brian was holding the puppy. He had slid down into the mud by this point, and was talking to the baby dog as he were a general giving orders to his troops. "My mom says we're not allowed to take one home."

Mr. Winter laughed a great belly laugh and placed two black puppies with shiny noses into my right arm. I cuddled them against my cheek. "They're not going anywhere yet. I think the whole lot will be my next team!"

Mr. Winter bred Iditarod dogs, and every year, with every litter, he expected that they'd all be good running dogs. He was the only man in our area to have won the Iditarod three times, and his family ran this farm the rest of the year, letting tourists pay to visit with the dogs and to walk through the makeshift museum he set up in another barn building toward the back of the estate.

"This one's your next lead!" Brian shouted, and raised the dog he was holding over his head.

"I think you're right!" he said. "Jessie, you two want to stay and help me with the next tour group?"

I checked my watch. Brian started jumping up and down. "Can we? Can we? Can we?"

"Oh, look, some of 'em are early." Mr. Winter

pointed to the driveway at the front of the house.

"Damn it!" Brian shouted.

"Brian!" I scolded, sounding like my mother. "I'm sorry, Mr. Winter. Brian, what is wrong with you?"

"You won't let us stay now."

I looked to the driveway, and sure enough, the car that had pulled in was a giant black Escalade, a car from out of town. The front door opened, and the blond goddess that was Evie descended from the passenger seat, followed by three miniature versions from the back of the car. Then, a man who wore a shiny suit and shoes that would get soaked from the snow made his way from the driver's side and locked the door of the car with the squeaky beeping sound from his key chain. He didn't look like any of my friends' dads. His hair was slicked back and he had one of those little phones in his ear and his teeth were unnaturally bright. I guessed this was Evie's father.

"Jessie! Hi!" Evie saw me and waved frantically. I didn't say anything, just smiled halfway and nodded my head at her. She came over to the edge of the pen and leaned against it.

"Do you work *here*, too?" she asked, puzzled.

Mr. Winter answered for me. "Nope. She just stopped by with Brian to see the pups." Then he walked out of the pen toward Evie's dad, who still stood by his car. I noticed that after he shook his hand, Mr. Stewart wiped it on a handkerchief he produced from his pants pocket.

Two of Evie's sisters hung back, hovering by their father, but another one, who was gap-toothed and freckly and about the same age as Brian, crowded around Evie's legs and began hanging on her. "Tiffany, get off!" she shouted. She wrenched her hand free of the girl.

"I want to go in!" the girl said demandingly.

"Fine, go. Geez." Evie pushed her toward the gate and the girl hopped it, like Brian had. She walked right over to Brian, who eyed her suspiciously.

"These are babies," he said to her. "You have to be quiet and patient."

She stuck her hands in the pockets of her

rainbow-embroidered denim jacket and said, "What do you think? I'm stupid?"

Evie and I watched this exchange carefully. "Tiffany!" Evie begged. "Be nice!"

The little girl wedged herself in next to my brother and commanded, "Show me." He looked at her sideways, then up at me for permission. I raised my shoulders in confusion. At that moment, I wouldn't have minded if he threw a fistful of dirt at the little girl. Because that's what I wanted to do to Evie, even though she'd always been nice to me. Going against all my brother's tactical instincts when it came to girls, he gingerly placed the puppy in Tiffany's lap and then picked up one of the puppy siblings and started pretending that it was attacking the others.

"Your brother's cute," Evie said to me.

I didn't say anything. What I wanted to say was "Are you going to try to steal him, too?" but I didn't. And I was a little proud of myself for my restraint.

"This place is amazing!" Evie went on. "Can you imagine living here year-round playing with puppies and dogs and deer and moose? Well, I guess you can, because you do live here year-round!"

I exhaled. Her happy tourist routine was seriously grating. "Yeah," I said, trying to make my voice sound friendly.

Evie must've sensed my quietness, because she bit her lip and then said to me in an entirely different tone, "Hey, listen, I hope we can be friends, okay?"

"Huh?"

"I mean, not that you need a new friend, I know you've got friends, and I mean, I may not be here for long—"

"That's right. This is just a vacation."

"Well, actually, my dad is buying one of the cabins, the empty one near the Reids'."

I nearly dropped the dogs I was holding. All this time, I thought that maybe this was a one-time visit, that maybe Evie would disappear from Jake's life once this trip was over.

"So we're going to be around more often. Which I can't wait for."

"Uh-huh."

"And I was just thinking that I'd like to

have some girlfriends to hang out with when I'm here."

"Oh," I said, dreading what was coming next.

"And you and Erin and Abby seem so cool, so, you know . . . I just wanted to say that I'd like to hang out with you."

"Well, er, I mean, Erin can be kind of, um, unsure about new friends."

Evie just looked at me. "Jessie, I know that you and Jake went out and everything."

My face did that funny hot thing it had done when Will mentioned kissing, and I put the dogs on the ground. She said "went out." Past tense. Which, I mean, hello? How stubborn was I that I would not acknowledge the fact that Evie was Jake's *new girlfriend*? I didn't say anything but I didn't seem to need to, what with Evie's running-at-the-mouth disorder.

"And I think it's really cool that you guys remained friends. And I think Will is really cool, and maybe it'd break the ice if we all went out together, like a double date."

"What? Will?"

"Yeah, you know, so that you won't feel weird around me anymore, and then we can all be friends."

I stared at her, unable to think of anything polite to say. It was just that I couldn't imagine anything that would make me feel weirder than going on a date with her and Jake. Wait. Yes, I could. And that would be going on a date with Will Parker.

"You cannot, cannot do that." Abby emphasized her point by slamming her fist onto the table.

It was later the same day, and I had called an emergency meeting of the troops to discuss whether or not to double-date.

"Whoa. Ab. Watch it there," Erin said, kidding our gentle friend who rarely displayed such a fiery temper.

We were at the Mountain Diner, the closest thing to a restaurant in Willow Hill. The diner wasn't on the resort premises; it was in the actual downtown area, which really wasn't much of anything. There was a post office here, and a small grocery store that looked like a house on the outside, and a hunting-and-camping/

outdoor-needs store. There was also a gas station, a pharmacy, and this diner. Willow Hill didn't have fast-food restaurants or chain stores or even a Wal-Mart. The girls and I would take a drive into Anchorage every week or so for a McNugget fix and a whirl around the aisles at the Kmart in town for kicks. And Evie thought this was such a great place! I'm pretty sure she could get McNuggets in Boise if she wanted to. I made a mental note to mention that the next time I was standing in awkward silence with her.

"I think you should go," Erin said, taking a fry off my mostly untouched plate.

"Why exactly?" I asked both of them, wanting to know their reasons for their opposing advice.

Erin gestured that Abby should make her case first. Abby began by also taking a fry from my plate. "It'll break your heart to have to sit there across the table and watch them all gooey-eyed over each other."

"Abby! I can handle that. It's nothing we haven't seen since they got here."

"She has some self-respect, Ab, or else she

wouldn't be all over Will Parker right now."

"Erin!"

"What?"

"How in any way am I all over him?"

She pointed at the coat I had worn to meet them—it was rolled up in the corner of the booth, but the large, red *X* was clearly visible.

"It's a *coat*, Erin. It's warmer than anything I have."

"Whatever. I respect it. He's way cuter than Jake anyway."

I looked at Abby out of habit, but she was looking past my shoulder to the doorway. Sabrina and Cam Brock were being shown to a table.

"Great," Abby whispered under her breath. She then shoveled a fistful of French fries into her mouth.

"Uck," Erin said. "You know what? We should get you a fake boyfriend too. Maybe when Jake leaves, Will can just move over to you."

"Will's not my fake boyfriend," I said.

"What do you think Evie thinks? Double date. She means with you and your new boyfriend."

I sipped a drink and thought about that.

"Besides, Jake's totally jealous, I can tell."

"How?"

Erin scooted closer to the table and beckoned Abby to lean in. "Okay. News. Today, when Agnes went on her break, you know, when she's gone for like an hour and then gets back and pretends that she only went to the ladies' room? Whatever."

"Just, what's the story?"

"Right. Well, I was behind the desk, and Jake came up, asking for a flyer for Mr. Winter's farm, you know, to check the schedule for the sled rides."

"But that makes no sense. Evie was already there."

"I know! I didn't think anything of this until just now. But I handed it to him and said, 'Jessie loves those dogs.'"

"Please tell me you didn't say that."

"Oh, I said it."

"Oh God." I dropped my head into my hands.

"Anyway, I said, 'Jessie loves those dogs,' and he looked at me funny, and said, 'Yeah. We took this sled ride once. I thought it might be a good thing to try again.'"

Abby and I just looked at Erin, who was grinning like she ate a whole pie in one sitting. "So? He's thinking about you."

I looked at Abby. "Erin, he was talking about Evie. About taking Evie."

"I don't think he was. He specifically said *you* had had such a great time out there."

I looked over at Sabrina and Cam.

"He's having buyer's remorse. I can tell. That guy's never satisfied with what he has."

I ignored this because Sabrina got up from her booth, and Cam caught my eye. Then, when Sabrina walked past us, she pinched me. "Ow!" I shouted. "What is your problem?" She didn't even look back or pretend she hadn't done it.

"Are you okay?" We looked up from our table, into the nut-brown eyes of Cam Brock. Abby squeaked.

"Um. Yeah," I said, shocked to see him there.

He shoved his hands in his pockets. "Yeah, um. Sorry about that."

"Okay," I answered, dumbfounded.

"Okay. Well, see you around. See you later, Abby."

And with that he was gone.

Poor Abby. I was scared to look at her, and when I did, it was as expected. Her eyes were all misty and her cheeks were pink and she wasn't breathing.

"Abby, back to earth," Erin commanded.

"Why did he say that? 'See you later, Abby.' Why did he say that?"

"He just did. Forget it," Erin commanded again.

Abby listened to Erin, but before she took another fry from my plate, she caught my eye and I knew that she hoped that Cam had come to talk to us because of her, not just because he had to apologize for his terrible girlfriend's behavior.

I walked home from the diner, even though the sun had completely disappeared and it was snowing lightly. Will's coat was remarkably warm, and I'd wrapped myself in a thick wool scarf that matched the hat I'd bought in Anchorage last year. My toes were sinking into the wintry chill, and I'd have been bothered by the wind hitting my face if my mind hadn't been so occupied by everything else.

It wasn't a far walk, really. We lived just over a mile from town, through the woods and past the path to the Winter farm. It was a walk I made often because I didn't have a driver's license. Now, I was walking because I wanted to sort things out in my head.

Erin sometimes didn't say things in the most tactful way, but she hardly ever exaggerated and never made things up. If she said that Jake was planning a sledding trip for us, then odds were good that he was. But this didn't make any sense to me. One day he was kissing me, then he avoided me for days. His family thought we were broken up and Evie clearly did too. I mean, we *were* broken up! And now what? He'd show up at my doorstep with eight dogs and a bouquet of flowers? It wasn't exactly his style.

Not to mention that every time I saw him and Evie together, they looked like they were really enjoying each other. I didn't know when I'd gone from the girlfriend to the other woman, but I'd gone from feeling special and happy to insecure and invisible.

I had to conclude that Erin was mistaken, and to trust my own mind. From what I saw, Jake wished I would go away. And maybe I should, I didn't know. I didn't want to make trouble, I wanted everything to just be settled. But on the other hand, I wanted explanations and apologies.

I just didn't know how I was going to get them. Maybe I *should* go on that double date with them. But that meant asking Will for another favor, and I didn't know if my insides could take it. He made me a little nervous.

God, if Sabrina had been in this situation, she would've locked Evie in her cabin, thrown away the key, and cornered Jake until he submitted. I kicked a foot full of snow in frustration. How exactly did good, nice girls get what they wanted? How had I gotten Jake in the first place?

I rewrapped the scarf around my neck, and thought about how excited Jake had been that first winter he was here. Maybe it was just as simple as this: that he'd been up here enough to know that there wasn't anything special about Willow Hill. Including me.

Chapter 9

When I woke the next morning, I sat up in bed and looked around my room at the empty wall. The day after we first saw Jake and Evie together, Erin had taken down each of Jake's pictures and packed all the gifts he'd given me into a box. I reached beneath my bed and felt around until I found the stack of pictures—Abby had rescued and organized them and hid them there for safekeeping. I shuffled through them once and then replaced them in their tomb.

He was my ex. He had a new girlfriend. Which meant he had no business kissing me, in his backyard or anywhere else. As I showered and got ready to go to Snow Cones, I thought to myself, *So what if I'll never get kissed again?* At least I knew what it was like. Wonderful.

But, other than the lack of kissing, what was *really* so bad about being single? I mean, really, Jake was my boyfriend by phone and text messages only. I had always gone to school alone and spent my summers alone. So really my life wouldn't be that different once the winter break was over. And the dance, I'd survive the dance. For one night, I'd be on the popular boy's arm, Sabrina would be driven crazy with jealousy, and all would be right with the world.

This was it. I was just going to make the best out of my new single life.

I stopped by Snow Cones on my way to Mount Crow and found Madison Reid at the counter with her mother.

"Jessie!" She leaped off the stool and flew into my arms. I picked her up with ease and carried her over to Mrs. Reid, who was drinking green tea. The woman was a stick. I'd be surprised if she'd ever tasted ice cream in her whole life.

"Hi, Mrs. Reid," I said to her.

"Hi, Jessie," she said warmly, taking Madison from me.

"How are you?"

"I'm good. I'm babysitting today." She pointed to the booth behind her, where I was surprised to see Evie's little sister sitting across from my brother, Brian. "I think little Tiffany has a crush."

I didn't even want to think about it.

"Are you working this morning?" she asked me.

"No, no, just stopped in for a pre-slope snack," I said, walking around the counter and resting against the shake machine.

"Okay, well, it's good to see you, Jessie," she said. "Come on, Tiff, we've got to go." Tiffany scrambled out of the booth, shouted, "Bye, jerk," to my brother, and bounded out the door.

"Bye, Jessie." Mad leaned across the counter and gave me a kiss on the cheek. Once they left, I made myself a special Single Jessie Goes Skiing concoction of rocky road and pistachio ice cream.

"Me too! I want some!" Brian came over and started eating from my dish.

"Who is that, your girlfriend?" I said snottily to him.

"At least I have one," he shot right back. I couldn't blame him.

I left Snow Cones and took Brian over to the slopes. We skied for about an hour, and then my mother picked him up to take him to hockey practice. I went back up, this time over to the hard trails, and began to run through a few hills. Erin was working, and Abby was too busy sewing my dress for the ball to come play with me. But I didn't mind. I had resolved to be a happy single girl. Single girls could ski without their friends and enjoy it.

I got into the chairlift line at the bottom of the hill. The line was long, much longer than any other time of year, because of the winter tourists. Families, teenagers, college kids— there were throngs of people waiting. It sometimes seemed kind of silly to me that you'd wait for up to a half hour to do something that lasted less than five minutes.

Just as I was congratulating myself on how

well I was handling my solitary lifestyle, I saw that Jake was walking toward me. He hadn't seen me yet, but I was sure that as soon as he did, he'd find a reason to turn the other way.

But I was tired of being ignored. And I didn't want to pretend not to see him. That's not what single girls who felt good about themselves did. So I waved my ski pole in the air and called out a sharp, pointed, "Hey."

He slowed when he saw me and there was a moment where I could see him deciding his next move. So I turned my back on him and paid attention to the line. I began a hard count in my head, "One pistachio, two pistachio," and promised that I wouldn't turn to see what direction he'd walked off in until I was at five pistachios.

Turns out, I didn't need to wait. Because I suddenly felt a jab in my side. "Hey," Jake said, standing right by me.

I lost my breath for a moment. I couldn't believe that he was openly engaging me in conversation.

"Hey," I said, wishing once again that I had just a little bit of Sabrina Hartley in me, just a little bit of an ability to say something cute and funny and fabulous.

"You holding a place for anyone?" He pointed to where I was standing in line, and actually, I think he kind of pointed at the red X on my coat.

"Nope, on my own today."

"No cutting, Jessica Whitman!" I turned behind me to see the small, hunched-over figure of Mean Agnes. She was wearing a pea-green parka over hot-pink leggings that she probably bought in kid's sizes—she wasn't an inch over four foot ten. Her lips were covered in bright red lipstick, and her skin was rouged as if she were a circus clown. I'd seen her skiing before. It wasn't a pretty sight.

"He's not cutting. I was waiting for him," I snapped right back.

"That's not what you just said." Mean Agnes harrumphed and accused me with her ski pole. "I'll be keeping my eye on you, missy!"

Jake looked at me with eyes rounded in mock horror. He could be so funny. I would miss the way he made me laugh.

"Don't sweat her," I whispered, trying not to laugh too hard.

Jake's smile was dazzling. "I'll be keeping my eye on you, missy."

I stopped laughing. He had broken up with me. I wasn't allowed to find anything he said funny anymore.

I pulled my goggles down over my eyes. I don't know why I did this. I normally hated wearing them—I liked to be able to see. But this easy conversation was making keeping my new resolutions difficult. In fact, I couldn't help wondering if he *was* going to ask me to go on a sled ride.

We moved forward, and Jake finally broke the silence. "Has the day been good?"

For a split second I contemplated not answering him, but that wouldn't accomplish anything. So I said, "Yeah. It's kind of icy over on the far hill. But here it's nice and smooth. You'll have a fast run."

"Cool," he said, and then we descended into silence. We didn't speak until we got to the very front of the line.

"Where's Evie today?" I asked. It wasn't even that I was trying to get the goods on him or bring up this sore subject, but we were being so quiet that it was getting awkward. I was desperate for conversation.

"Oh, um. You know. At the spa again. Skiing's not her thing."

I looked at him then and made a face. "This town is even more boring if skiing's not your thing. What will she do every year? Just go to that spa?"

He looked at me funny.

"I mean, I know that her family is buying a cabin here or whatever."

"Oh," he said. "I told her she'd like it better in the summer, when she could see all the animals and the trees and stuff. I don't think she will, though."

"You don't think she will what?"

"I don't think she'll like it at all." That was it! Proof! He was over Willow Hill! This actually made me feel a little bit better. I mean, I couldn't help where I was from, right?

Thankfully we were next in line, so I didn't have to say anything more to him. I'd run out of topics that would preserve my newfound single dignity and I didn't want him to say or do anything else that would remind me how good we were together. Before I knew it we were in the air in our chair, our skis dangling from our feet over the treetops and building roofs. I took a deep breath and let the cold winter air into my lungs.

When we got to the top of the mountain, I readjusted my goggles and pulled my hat down tighter over my head. I wasn't sure what to expect here. I didn't know if Jake had just ridden with me to get an earlier spot in line.

But he pointed his ski pole at me and then at the bottom of the hill. "Heard you were the slowest skier out here!" And then he pushed himself down in a gathering of speed and the chase was on!

I pushed myself forward and then gravity took over. I went hurtling over moguls and cutting in and out of the ski paths, keeping my eye on him the whole time. He was about ten feet in front of me, and I knew that there was a turn coming up that I could take advantage of. Sure enough, when there was about a third of the hill left for us, I cut my skis to the left, and pushed myself forward. Then I jammed my body to the right, and I overtook him.

He screamed, "Hey! Not fair!" as I streaked past him to the bottom of the hill.

I raised my poles high over my head in victory.

Jake finally skied to where I was and came to a stop in front of me. "Not fair! You have a home team advantage!" He whipped the goggles off his head and grinned at me.

I grinned back. "Double or nothing."

"You're on." He immediately turned and made his way to the chairlift, replacing his goggles on his head.

I skied behind him, grinning from ear to ear. Being single wasn't nearly as fun as skiing with Jake.

We spent the whole day together. By the time we trudged into the lodge, the sun had set, and the ski lights were on and I was right back where I started, wanting to be his girlfriend again. My face was red and cold—I probably looked like a big shiny apple—but I didn't care. This was what I had needed. A day with Jake, to remind him that I was fun and interesting and that we could have a future outside of this town. "Want a hot chocolate? My treat, since I won most of the races." We were standing in the doorway of the lodge, and the warmth of the room was making my fingers tingle.

Jake didn't answer. I don't think he heard me. He was scanning the room, and I assumed that he was looking for Evie. I looked around the room too. There were a lot of people there, people like us who'd finished their day's runs and were looking to warm up.

But no Evie.

Jake didn't answer. So I poked him with my pole. "Hot chocolate? On me?"

He looked at me finally, and mumbled, "Okay."

I went to the counter, where I recognized the girl working, the girl who had looked so smitten by Will Parker the other day. She was a friend of Erin's from the resort. She went to college in Anchorage but came back home to work during weeks like this when it was so busy.

I watched her make my hot chocolates and tried to think about what to do next. How to keep these good feelings going? We had had a fun time, and it was like it used to be, us skiing, laughing as we raced. We'd even taken a break and sat in the snow at the base of the hill, by the sledding tracks, and watched the kids race one another on souped-up, homebuilt sleds. I quickly retrieved my cell phone from the inner pocket of my parka, and texted Erin.

FAVOR: CHECK SPA LOG. WHEN DOES RIVAL GET DONE?

The girl handed me my hot chocolates and I blew on them. The steam rising from the white whipped cream meant that we wouldn't be able to drink them too soon. I checked my cell phone, willing Erin to get my message before Jake saw that the drinks were ready. Lo and behold, my friend came through:

ONE HOUR. GODSPEED!

I grabbed the handles on the mugs and weaved my way through the crowds to where Jake was sitting on a couch right in front of the fire. One hour was all I had to make him fall for me again, make him realize it was better to have a girlfriend with his interests. I mean, what, was he going to ski alone whenever he and Evie were at Mount Crow?

I handed him the mugs, unzipped Will's

parka, and sat. The ends of my pigtails were frozen and tickled my neck.

He handed me my mug and we both sipped, or tried to.

"Sorry, they're a little hot," I said to him, but I kept looking at the fire. Skiing was one thing, but now, sitting next to him, I didn't know what to say. I snuck a peek at him. Yup. He was the same old Jake, with his tan skin and his cute brown mole on his cheek. His hair was sweaty and mussed up from our day. He held the mug near his chin and looked at me. He smiled.

I smiled back.

Then he breathed in deeply. I did the same. Then, finally, I couldn't take it anymore—I began to giggle, a terribly childish trait of mine. This broke the ice, though, and he put down his mug and poked me in the side. This sent me into catastrophic peals of laughter.

"I forgot how ticklish you are!" he said.

I put my hot chocolate on the table in front of me and turned with raised hands to play defense.

"Stop it!" I squealed, doubled over to fend off his ticklish advances.

"Nope! Winner's prize is tickles!" He kept at it, until finally the women sitting behind us, on a couch that was back-to-back with ours, turned and shushed us.

Jake and I looked at each other conspiratorially.

"Sorry. Sorry," I said to the ladies, and Jake had to bend over to keep himself from laughing.

"You're such a troublemaker," he teased, grabbing my hand.

And then this broke the giggle spell. He held on to my hand and I looked at him, and then it all came rushing back. All my hurt feelings about him and Evie and the memory of him kissing me in his backyard.

I think he sensed that my mood changed, but he didn't let go of my hand.

"Jessie, I had a good day with you. I forgot about how fun it was."

Who needed one whole hour? Mission accomplished in five minutes! I was *so* the champion!

I looked at our hands in my lap, and then felt him move in closer to me. My heart started pounding. Was he going to kiss me again?

Kisses at nighttime when nobody was looking was one thing, but kisses in daytime in public were quite another! For a split second I thought of Will and how I'd have to tell him our date for the dance was off.

And then the moment was broken before it could start, because we suddenly heard someone shouting, "Jake? Jake?"

Jake dropped my hand and quickly put distance between us. Evie stood in the doorway. Her hair was shiny and styled, and her eyes were bright as she scanned the room. When she finally saw us, she smiled broadly and marched over to the couch.

"Hey! Were you skiing?" she asked, and I thought that it was the dumbest question ever. I also thought that she looked a little too brown.

"Were you tanning?" I asked, topping her dumb question with one of my own.

"Oh! Yes! I was supposed to get a massage, but I ditched it for this fun little tanning booth in town. The old woman at the front desk suggested it." Evie plopped herself down in between us, and reached for Jake's hot chocolate. "Is this yours?" she asked him with no time for him to answer before she took a long drink from it.

Mean Agnes struck again! She sent Evie to her sister's tanning salon and robbed me of an hour of kissing Jake in front of the fire!

Evie began to babble about the town and how quaint it was (God, I hated that description) while I cursed Mean Agnes mentally, even though I should've been cursing Evie. Actually, scratch that. I should have been cursing Jake. How dare he be holding my hand when he had this other girl wandering around the town, thinking they were boyfriend and girlfriend? Erin's voice echoed in my head, *I think Jake will kiss whoever's in front of him.* I drowned it out by gritting my teeth.

My head started to pound. I reached for my hot chocolate and felt Jake's eyes on me. I caught them and he didn't look away. His face was so earnest, he couldn't possibly have been thinking about Evie and what she was talking about. Who knew there was this much to say about tanning beds?

Then Evie said, "So, I found this cute little

diner. Why don't we go there for our double date?"

Jake choked on his hot chocolate. "Double date?"

"Yes, silly, didn't I tell you? We're going on a double date. I thought it'd be fun."

Jake looked at me, panicked. And this for some reason made me happy. He deserved to be a little panicky.

"Yup. Tons of fun, right, *Jakey*?" I asked.

He squinted his eyes at me. I smiled brighter.

"So, Jessie, can you and Will do it tomorrow night? At that diner place?"

"You and Will?" Jake asked.

"Oh, of course!" I exclaimed brightly. "You mean the Mountain Diner. Will and I love that place."

"Yes! The Mountain Diner! Sooo *cute*!" I had to stop myself from rolling my eyes. Like there weren't *diners* in Boise.

But one thing I had learned from my day, I couldn't just give up. Jake was on the fence. He'd forgotten how much fun we could have together, but today had reminded him. Now, by my calculation, one good dose of jealousy, and I'd get him back.

I decided to quit while I was ahead. I told the two of them that I'd see them later, that I was meeting Will. (I flat-out lied. This whole situation was making me a bad person!)

I walked away and blew Jake a kiss when Evie wasn't looking. Then I ran down the path, wondering how in the world I was going to talk Will Parker into going on another date with me.

Chapter 10

"*H*ave you seen Will?"

Erin stood at the front desk in the Mount Crow hotel lobby, leaning forward and reading her book. She looked up and arched an eyebrow. "No. Why?"

I sighed and bit my lip. "Double date. I agreed to go."

Erin flipped her book closed and smiled broadly. "That's the spirit. Make him jealous."

I took off my coat and hat and gloves and handed them to her.

"This coat weighs a hundred pounds." I could hear her but couldn't see her. Will's coat was obstructing her from view. She waddled away and threw all my stuff on a chair behind her. She walked back to me and produced a book from beneath the desk. The words INSTRUCTOR SCHEDULE were written across the front in the scratchy hieroglyphics of Mean Agnes. She flipped a few pages and then dragged her finger down the page. "He's teaching. He'll be done in about an hour. So, tell me where we stand."

"Where we stand, where we stand," I said, taking a butterscotch candy from the dish on the table. "Well, we spent yesterday skiing."

Erin's eyebrows shot up to her hairline. "You did? That's fantastic. Did Sabrina see you?"

"No," I said, annoyed. "Me and *Jake*."

"Oh," she said flatly. "Let me guess. You had a great time and then the minute he saw Evie, it was like you didn't exist."

"No!" I said snottily, even though, really, um, yes.

"You're a terrible liar." Erin snorted, and reopened her novel.

"How do I ask Will to do this?"

"Just ask. He'll go. He's cool about that stuff."

"Yeah, yeah. You're right." But I couldn't

figure out why I felt so nervous about asking him.

Mean Agnes chased me out of the lobby, or else I would have passed the hour happily with Erin, procrastinating. For some reason, the thought of approaching Will and basically asking him out on a date was making me nauseous. But Mean Agnes cared not for my teenage angst and so I found myself wandering through the grounds of the resort, trudging through the snow from one mountain to another.

With each footstep, my stomach rumbled. I'd never noticed that Will made me this uncomfortable before. I tried to remember whether my stomach flipped when I'd see him in the halls of Willow High, but I didn't think so. Maybe it was because I'd never really had anything to say to him before, and now, the entirety of my happiness was held in his hands.

I finally found him. He was coaching two upper-middle-class couples how to snowboard on the far hill, the one that was out of the way and had the gentlest slopes of all the mountains. He caught my eye while I was leaning against the fence, and winked at me. My stomach began flopping around like a fish. I waved at him, then turned immediately and walked away. I didn't want him to think I was waiting for him, even though I *was* waiting for him. I was so caught up in thinking how strange I was behaving that I barely noticed that I was now standing at the base of the sledding peak. Also, I failed to notice the two inner tubes careening around like bumper cars, the people on them steering so that they were ramming into each other. In fact, I didn't notice them until they were closer to the bottom of the mountain. I wondered if I should get Will so he could tell them to knock it off. That's when I saw that they were gunning for one of Evie's little sisters, who was on a tube of her own and looked terrified to be going as fast as she was. Sure enough the little girl was hit from behind by one of the careening tubes, and as I heard the cackle of laughter, I also heard a sound coming from the other inner tube—the sound of my brother making blowup noises.

I stood there fuming, only to become a target in my own right.

Over the whining of the overturned sister,

my brother shouted his orders to Tiffany. "Get Jessie! Get Jessie!"

I couldn't get out of the way fast enough. Brian had set his sights on me and was moving like a bullet. "Yah! Yah!" Tiffany shouted. Soon enough I felt myself go down, cut off at the knees by my brother and his annoying girlfriend.

"Ow!" I shouted, and tried to punch Brian in the back. "You're such a little —"

"You missed! You missed!" He jumped up, helped Tiffany to her feet, and then ran away with her, each of them laughing and running with their inner tubes for their dear lives.

"I'm going to kill you!" I shouted from where I lay on the ground. I breathed out in complete frustration.

Before I could help myself up, Will Parker was leaning down next to me, pulling me up by my hands. "Hey there, killer, you okay?"

"If Brian ever disappears, you know who to ask about it," I spat out.

"Kids do that all day long here," Will said. He was kneeling beside me and had his hands on my arms. "You okay? You get the breath knocked out of you?"

He was looking at me with the most emotion I'd ever seen on his face before. He was usually so cool and collected. I'd never imagined that he'd be good in a crisis.

"Anything broken?" Now he was smiling and poked me in the ribs. I smiled back at him.

"No, I'm okay. Just embarrassed to take a spill in front of everybody."

"Ah, no one cares," he said. Then he stood on his feet in a crouch and began to help me to my feet.

I felt light-headed for a minute and was rocking on my feet a bit. Will's hands moved around to my back, and he held me up for a moment. I felt embarrassed all over again.

"Come on. Let's get you some ice cream," he said, and helped me walk across to Snow Cones, his arm around me the whole way.

When we got there, my mother was standing in the doorway waiting. "What happened?"

"Your son is a demon!" I choked out.

"Just some good clean fun, Mrs. Whitman," Will said. Once we stepped into Snow Cones, I shrugged away from his arm, which was still around me. I felt funny with my mother there, and suddenly realized how silly I was being. I was fine. I could certainly walk. "She hit her head good, though."

My mother narrowed her eyes at me and pursed her lips. "Okay. You two sit over there."

Will and I slid into a booth and I took a breath.

"Okay?" he asked me.

"Yeah. He won't live to see thirteen."

Will laughed and started fiddling with the salt shaker. "At least my coat broke your fall."

I smiled, feeling self-conscious. Also, my stomach was feeling unsettled again. "I don't know why I keep wearing it. I'm sorry."

I began to take it off, but Will reached across the table and stopped me. "No, you keep it. No worries."

I zipped it back up and drummed my fingers on the table.

"So, what were you doing there anyway?" he asked, after my mother brought us some ice cream.

"Oh." In the aftermath of being run over, I'd

forgotten all about the double date. Now that I remembered, my stomach started doing somersaults all over again.

"You mind?" He reached for my dish, and after I nodded, took a spoonful of my Chocolate Fiesta. "Spicy."

"Yeah," I said, pushing it toward him. "Um, listen. I feel really horrible."

"Yeah?"

"Um, yeah. Um. I think, well—"

"Dude. Are you proposing? 'Cuz I think we're too young." He looked at me seriously at first, then broke into a grin that was nothing short of dazzling.

I bit my lip because I'd never been so mortified in my life. My stomach was doing the rumba and I felt like I could hear the blood pumping in my veins. I took a deep breath, gathered my courage by staring briefly down into my lap, and looked him in the eye. "Okay. Listen. Evie and Jake think we're, um—"

"Together?"

"Yes." I held my breath waiting for his reaction but all he did was raise his shoulders.

"'Kay," he said.

I stared at him. Nothing ever bothered him. "'Kay? That's it? 'Kay?"

"What do you want me to say?"

I sighed. Now I was getting annoyed. "Nothing. They think we're, you know, together, and they want to go on a double date with us tomorrow. Just say no, and I'll get out of it."

He pointed at me. "I'm saying yes."

"Really?"

"Yup. We'll call it a trial run, so I know what to expect out of you at the dance."

I sat back in the booth's bench and surveyed him. He was dipping his spoon into each of our dishes and eating his concoctions without looking at me. I had no idea what life would be like if you were somebody like him, somebody who really didn't care about anything. Just then, he noticed that I was watching him and raised the spoon with the double flavors to me. "You wanna try?"

"I'm good."

"Come on," he taunted, pushing the spoon practically to my face.

I relented and took the bite.

"Good, right?"

I shook my head. "Yeah, but I think it's just my concussion confusing my taste buds."

"Nah," he laughed. "Whitman, I'll never steer you wrong."

Chapter 11

"I'm not wearing that!" I pushed the black smock back toward Erin. It was the night of the dreaded double date, and the girls were at my house helping me pick an outfit.

"What's wrong with it?" Erin asked, waving the sequined, netted frock in the air. She had brought what she had referred to as the "perfect date outfit."

"She'll look like the angel of death, that's what's wrong with it," Abby replied as she stepped into my closet to survey my clothes. "Gosh, you really do have nothing to wear."

"I know, I know," I said glumly. Who knew that I could be this discerning about my clothes? But every shirt, skirt, or pair of pants that Abby selected out of my closet seemed boring and unexciting. I mean, I was going out with *Will*

Parker. Fake date or no, I couldn't show up looking like, well, like myself.

"I told you that you have too many flannel shirts," Erin chimed in from behind us.

"*You* didn't say that! *I* said that!" Abby argued.

"Geesh. Whoever. She has too much flannel. It's not good date material." I *did* have lots of flannel. And lots of denim and boots and other clothes that would look great on construction workers.

"Well, I'm not wearing that black fishnetty thing. If my mother saw me in that I'd be grounded until I was twenty-five."

Abby touched my arm. "When she's not looking, let's grab it and burn it."

"I can hear you, you know!" Erin responded. Since her clothing offer was turned down, she situated herself on my rocking chair and pulled from her bag the same thick book she'd been reading at the lodge.

"How many pages is that?" I asked.

"A thousand," she replied proudly.

Abby smiled as we left Erin to her reading

and continued to survey the contents of my closet. Abby constantly reminded me that she'd give her right hand, her sewing hand, for a walk-in closet like this. Staring inside it, I felt completely unworthy of both this closet and of this fake date.

Abby blew air out of her mouth and said, "Okay. We're going to have to raid my house. Erin, you coming with?"

We stepped out of the closet, and Erin looked up at us. She hadn't been listening.

"Nah, I'll stay here."

What was weirder than Erin volunteering to stay at *my* house was the fact that Will Parker was sitting at my kitchen table, talking to my father. At the sight of him, I stopped dead in my tracks, which caused Abby to walk right into me. Will and my father looked up at us like we were a couple of clods.

"There's my favorite girl," my father bellowed.

"You okay there, Whitman?" Will asked.

I looked at him. His blond hair gleamed in the darkness of our kitchen. It was shorter than it had been the last time I'd seen him and I had a fleeting thought that he'd cut it just for our date. Then I realized I was staring and wished with all my might that the floor would open and swallow me up.

Abby giggled as she regained her footing. "Hiya, Mr. Whitman."

Will sat up straighter in his chair. "Your dad and I were just talking about you."

Abby turned to me with an expectant expression on her face, and I purposely ignored her, suddenly fearing that Will had woken up, realized he was doing me too many favors, and was here to break the news that he was bailing on me. "Everything still okay?" I asked cautiously.

"Of course," he admonished, shooing my concerns away with his hand. As he looked at me, I could see his smile disappear. "Is that what you're wearing tonight?"

I looked down at my outfit. Flannel and denim. Again, I prayed silently for the floor to give way so that I could disappear. "No, um, we're going out now. I'll be ready in time."

I mumbled this last part, and I could feel

my father looking from Will to me and back to Will again.

"Jessica, Will here was asking if I could fly him up to Grizzly Mountain in a couple of days."

Abby grabbed an apple from the counter and headed to the table, where she sat next to Will. "What's Grizzly Mountain?"

Will scoffed at her. "Only the best powder in the whole Northern Hemisphere. Right, Mr. Whitman?"

"He's right."

I looked at my dad in surprise. He wasn't usually in the business of flying kids up to their favorite skiing spots.

"You don't understand," Will began, and as he continued to talk he got more and more animated. "There's gonna be this huge storm there the next couple of days, but when it clears, there's going to be, like, twelve feet of powder. It'll be sick. We can't miss it."

Abby caught my eye then, and I realized why my dad was willing to do this favor for a friend of mine. He thought he was helping mend my broken heart.

"We can't?" I squeaked.

"Nope. You and me." He motioned back and forth between us. "It'll be the best time ever. So, it's cool, Mr. Whitman?"

My father walked to where I stood and rustled my hair. I tried to avoid it but he was too fast for me. "Just has to be before Thursday." Thursdays were the days he flew up to the Arctic Circle on supply runs. Otherwise, my dad had a lot of free time.

"Awesome." Will stretched until his chair tipped onto its two back legs. "Basically, you and I are going to have the best winter break week ever."

Abby again looked at me with a mischievous and expectant face.

I could hear the blood rushing to my head again. I was so confused; I didn't say anything right away. "Um, well, Abby and I gotta go. But you'll be back in a couple of hours?"

Will smiled at me. "You got it."

Abby's closet was entirely different from mine, as I knew it would be. By the time we'd sorted through outfits and picked possible combinations, I was feeling like myself again. My stomach was normal and my pulse wasn't loud enough for the neighbors to hear. And carrying all the skirts and soft-colored shirts and pretty earrings made me excited. Abby would make me look good, maybe good enough to get Jake to look at me once in a while. And good enough that Will wouldn't crack jokes about me to Sabrina and Cam and Jay after our date.

When the two of us finally fell into my front foyer an hour after we'd left, laden down with bundles of borrowed items, the house was quiet and only one or two lights were on. "Hello?" I called out in the darkness.

Nobody answered, but after a moment, I could hear the screams and thuds of my brother, which meant he was in the throes of some major video-game-playing action. Throwing down the piles of clothes onto the table by the stairs, Abby and I wandered into the back room, where the television was.

In the room were Brian, his little friend Tiffany, who was in denim overalls and a pink frilly shirt, Erin, and Will, whose shoes were kicked off. All four of them were fully focused on the television.

"Hey, guys." Erin tore her gaze away, but only very briefly. She was seated on the couch next to Will. "Successful mission?"

Abby plopped herself down on my father's overstuffed lounge chair. "Mission accomplished."

"What's going on?" I finally asked suspiciously.

Will was half standing and half sitting on our couch, his body contorting in mimicry of the bending and twirling motions his on-screen flying fighting contraption was making. "Huh? What? Oh, hey, Whitman," he said. "Take that, you little thug!" he shouted at Brian. Tiffany squealed in support of my brother.

"Just some high-octane competition," Erin responded.

My brother didn't seem to be offended by Will's attack. In fact, he was screaming and jumping up and down halfway between the couch and the television. He and Will were operating two flying machines that were engaged in heated nose-to-nose combat, while Tiffany tried to coach Brian on how to maneuver.

"Hey! How do you do that flippie thing?" Will asked Brian while I stood there, trying to figure out why I was so irritated at this scene.

"Press this button," Brian said. He didn't even stop jumping. He just leaned over and pressed the proper button on Will's controller.

Will shouted, "Aha! You're dead!"

Erin cheered and high-fived him.

"Will!"

That broke the spell. He turned to me while Brian yelled, "Jessie, we're playing a game. Go away!"

Will said at practically the same time, "Oh, yeah, hey. Just come down when you're ready and we'll go."

I opened my mouth to respond but no words came out. I was so shocked by the sight of Will in my living room, and Erin playing video games, and Brian with a friend over who was a girl, I couldn't process it all. So I did what Will suggested. I turned on my heel and stomped up the two sets of stairs to my room. I was trailing clothes behind me, and Abby had to keep stopping to pick them up.

"Jessie! What's wrong with you?" she asked, throwing the piles of clothes onto the bed.

I began sorting through them all, organizing the clothes into proper piles: shirts, skirts, pullovers.

"Jess?" Abby asked again.

"Nothing's wrong." I sat on my bed. The truth was that something was niggling at me but I wasn't sure what.

Abby pulled a pale pink button-down shirt and a brown tulip skirt from the piles. "I think you should go with these. This shirt will bring out your eyes."

I looked at the outfit and nodded. "Okay."

"Okay," Abby agreed. When I didn't make a move to get up, she tilted her head. "So?"

"So nothing." I stood and took the clothes from her. "Would you tell me if Erin liked Will?"

My question shocked Abby. It shocked me! She shook her head in confusion. "Is that what this is about? You're worried about Erin and Will? I thought you wanted them to go out."

I could feel my face reddening. "I do. I mean, I thought I did."

Abby smiled a small, suspicious smile. "Hmmm."

I sat back down on the bed and propped myself up on my elbows. "Stop. I'm just nervous about tonight is all. I'm nervous that he's not going to take it seriously."

Abby sat next to me. "Of course he's going to take it seriously. Didn't you see how dressed up he was?"

I sat up again. "He was?"

"Don't you notice anything?"

"I'm juggling a real ex-boyfriend with a fake new boyfriend! These kinds of machinations can distract a girl!"

Abby sighed. "I think he looks really nice. He has on new pants. And I've never seen that long-sleeved shirt before. And I'm pretty sure he washed his hair."

"How could you possibly tell that?"

She shrugged. "I know these things. And, I mean, that whole Grizzly Mountain thing? That's a second date he's planning."

My stomach did that flippy thing again. "You think?"

"What else could it be?"

A second date. That couldn't be right. I took the outfit from Abby and walked into my closet to change, thinking about Grizzly Mountain the entire time. It was kind of a weird thing to plan for just me. Right? My stomach launched into its flipping sequence just thinking about being in a tiny airplane with only Will and my father.

It wasn't until I was watching Abby style my hair in the mirror that I remembered the whole point of the night: Jake.

Chapter 12

*A*n hour later, Will and I were walking along the path from my house to the main road, which would lead right to the diner.

"We should've taken my scooter," he said for the twelfth time.

"Stop. We're walking. It's nicer," I said, but what I meant was that I didn't want to ride on his scooter for a mile, with him right there in front of me.

Abby was right. Will *did* look good. I'd never really allowed myself to *notice* before because it did no good to think about Will Parker like that. But now, as we walked, my mind kept wandering. A new fantasy had sprung up in fantasyland, and it took place right here in Willow Hill, in school, no less. I was fantasizing about what it would be like to be in class with Will when school started back up again. I wondered if he'd talk to me as much as he seemed to be doing this break. I was very conscious of the fact that he sat right next to me in English, something I'd never thought twice about before.

Also, I was uncomfortable because my heart was beating really loudly. I could hear it in my own ears. I couldn't even pretend that it was because of the high wire I was going to be walking at the big date, because it started when Will had knocked on my bedroom door a half an hour before we were to meet Jake and Evie. When he saw me, he whistled.

He actually whistled!

Now we were walking down the path and I was spying on him. Like I said, Abby was right. His jeans were new, but they looked broken in. He had on the sneakers that he always wore, which were casual and cool and made him look like he didn't care too much—this was the look that had slain Sabrina and so many other girls in my school. And his hair wasn't only washed.

"Did you get a haircut?" I asked, before

I could stop the words from flying out of my mouth.

He turned to me as we walked. "Yup. You like?" And he ran a hand through his hair and struck a pouty-lipped pose.

I laughed and kept walking, and tried to breathe deeply to steady my heart rate. It *had* to be nerves. I didn't like Will Parker. I liked *Jake*. Maybe it was the thing that actors and actresses go through when they are pretending to be married in a movie and fall in love for real, only to break up as soon as the movie is over.

"So, tonight," I said.

"Yeah. It's gonna be wild."

"I think we should set some ground rules."

"Yeah?"

"Yeah."

"Okay. Ground rule one. No macking on Jake right in front of me."

I looked at him, startled.

"What?" he asked. "We're playing roles, right? No macking on Jake. That'd make you a bad girlfriend."

"Oh," I said, and peeked at him. I couldn't

tell if he was giving me a serious message. "Okay, well, no macking on Evie."

"Why would I do that?" he asked, his voice sounding serious.

"I don't know. I just thought, you know, I'm matching you, rule for rule."

He stopped walking. "What's the point here?"

"Huh?"

"The point. Of tonight?"

"Oh. I don't know. Evie wanted to do this. I guess just to get through it."

"Um-hmm."

"You know, and make Jake realize I'm the better girl for him."

Will looked away for a minute and raised his shoulders to his chin. I didn't know what the gesture meant. "Okay. I got it."

And then he walked forward and I had to catch up. While we walked, I kept trying to picture how I would behave in front of Jake and Evie, but instead all I could think about was the trip to Grizzly Mountain. Again, I pictured the two of us in my father's plane and got the stomach flips. I shook my head to clear it; I tried to think about Jake.

"You okay?" Will had stopped walking.

"Huh?"

"We're here." Will gestured behind him. I had been so wrapped up in my thoughts I hadn't realized that we were standing on the street opposite of the restaurant. I turned to Will.

"Ready?" I asked.

He reached out to touch my hair. I tried to duck. "What the—?"

He pulled a fuzzy piece of dandelion from my hair and held it up. "Just cleaning you up a bit."

"Oh. Okay. Sorry. Do I look good now?" I held out my arms and did a mini half-twirl.

His eyes squinted. "Like a million bucks."

Then he grabbed me by the hand and charged across the street.

His hand was warm, even though it was twenty degrees outside and he hadn't been wearing gloves on our walk. I felt momentarily embarrassed by the fact that my hands were ice-cold. As we approached the door, I tried to pull my hand from his.

"What's wrong?" He turned to me, not letting go.

"It's just . . ." I pointed to the picture window of the diner. "What if kids from school are in there?"

"So?" He was still holding my hand. And then he shook his head, like he really didn't care.

I tried to pull it away again, to no avail. "I just—" I held up our clasping hands. "What if someone sees?"

He looked at me like I had twelve heads. "So?" Then he pulled the door open and we walked inside.

The first thing I saw was Sabrina and the Clique of Satan at the choice corner booth, the one with the wraparound bench and the cozy lighting. Her hair was piled on her head like a 1960s movie star and she was wearing a silk print top that seemed like something she borrowed from her mother. Her lips were covered in pink lip gloss. Sitting next to her was Cam, who was idly playing with a spoon. Stephanie and Hannah were there too, bending across the table, hanging on Sabrina's every word.

She was mid-sentence when she caught sight of Will and me. The French fry she was holding fell to the table.

I couldn't help it. I smiled. Sabrina's eyes were wide and her mouth was pursed, and the Clique of Satan looked scared to say *anything* to her. I wanted to jump and shout that *this* was what it felt like to steal other girls' crushes.

Will saw exactly what I saw and whispered in my ear, "See? Good times."

"Parker!" Cam shouted, and waved at us.

Will pulled me toward them, still holding my hand. My hand had now warmed up. I was growing very conscious of the fact that it was getting sweaty.

"Parker!" Cam shouted again. This time he backhand-slapped Will. I didn't know what was up with these boys and last names.

"What's up, kids?" Will asked the table of people. Sabrina was boring holes into me with her eyes. I tried to position myself behind Will to avoid her death-ray hate stare.

"What are you guys doing?" Sabrina asked

finally, seething. Her teeth were clenched so hard I thought they were going to fall out of her head.

"Yeah, you guys want to join up?" Cam pushed farther into the booth, making room for us. "Jessie, is a, um, are your friends coming tonight?"

Will looked at me as I didn't answer right away, and when I did, my voice sounded like there was a frog in it. "Oh, um, no, we're, um—" and I looked over my shoulder, trying to see if Evie and Jake were in the diner. They were, in the opposite corner of this cool-kid booth.

"Yeah, we gotta thing we gotta do," Will announced. He was *still* holding my hand. And Sabrina looked like she wanted to cry. Part of me started to feel bad, but then she clamped down on Cam's shoulder and glared at me. "We'll catch you later, Brock." Then Will and Cam backhand-slapped each other again, and Will finally began walking toward Evie and Jake, pulling me behind him.

"Will!"

"Yeah?" He looked at me over his shoulder.

I opened my mouth to ask him to stop

pulling me but couldn't say anything. His hair was blinding.

"No worries. It'll be good. C'mon. Let's sell it." And then he made a face at me, a face that Jake and Evie wouldn't have been able to see. He drew his eyes toward his nose and stuck his tongue out. It was so goofy. I couldn't help myself. I started to laugh.

"There you go. Drive him mad, babe!"

We finally got to the table, and Jake stood up. He was wearing dark blue jeans and a long-sleeved black T-shirt. His hair was brushed to the side, flopping just over his left eye. I wondered what that meant. He never did his hair like that. Actually, *I* used to style it like that when I was trying to tease him.

"Hey, man," Will said to him, and held out his hand so he could do that weird-boy slap thing. Jake just looked at Will's hand, which was suspended in midair.

"Um, hi, guys," I said.

"Wow! You look great!" Evie said, reaching out to touch my skirt. "Love this fabric!"

"It's my frie—" Will elbowed me in the side. "Ow!" I said. He made a face at me. I understood what he was trying to say. "It's my favorite," I finished up, and took my seat.

"So I ordered appetizers. Does everyone like appetizers?" Evie sat straight-backed, two inches from the support of the booth, passing out menus. She was like a cruise director in training. Perky and pleasant and organizing everything.

"Jake, what's up, man? How's the skiing?" Will slung his arm over my shoulder and moved in closer to me. Jake caught my eye and then shifted his gaze to Will's arm. As if he saw this, Will dropped his hand onto my shoulder and started rubbing it in a circle.

Jake narrowed his eyes, and put *his* arm around Evie. In return I snuggled into Will's side, which was a bad idea because it sent my stomach onto a roller-coaster track. I tried to disengage but Will wouldn't let me. His grip on my shoulder was like iron.

I looked at Jake. He looked at me.

Then Evie started up again with her activities directing. "So, I can't believe how you all know how to ski! I told Jake that I'm no good to him this far north."

"You don't ski?" Will asked, looking at me for confirmation.

I nodded. "She likes the spa."

"The spa? Are you crazy? You're missing out!"

Evie dipped her lashes and began to blush. I'd seen this look before: It appeared on girls of all ages when they talked to Will. He was like girl catnip.

Will began to describe to her what hitting a perfect powdery hill was like, and her blush deepened. While he talked, he noticeably tapped my shoulder with his fingers. It was like we were communicating without words. He was letting me know that I should talk to Jake while he monopolized Evie's time.

But Jake wasn't looking at me. He was studying the menu like it was in Greek. So I kicked him under the table.

"Ouch!" Jake said.

"Are you okay?" Evie asked, tearing her gaze away from Will for two seconds.

"Yeah, yeah, it's nothing," Jake replied,

and made a face at me, a face that demanded to know why I'd kicked him.

"Sorry," I mouthed to him, and leaned across the table. "Sorry."

"What's going on?" he asked quietly.

"Nothing." I swallowed hard. It was in this moment that I'd wished I'd formulated a game plan instead of spending so much time falling prey to Will's mojo. "Just, hey, you want to go skiing with me tomorrow?" I tried to say this softly enough that Evie couldn't hear, but of course that was stupid. I mean, she was sitting a foot from us!

"Hey!" she interrupted. "I have a great idea! Why don't the four of us go? And you"—she nodded at Will—"could teach me."

"I have an even better idea," Will said.

"You do?" I asked.

"Yeah. They should come to Grizzly Mountain."

"What? They should?" Now I felt like someone had kicked *me*, but in the stomach and not gently.

"Yeah, they should. Her dad's a pilot. He's gonna fly us up to Grizzly Mountain. It's got the best skiing in the state," Will explained to Jake and Evie.

Evie's face lit up. Jake's fell.

"Jake's afraid of flying. He won't go up in my dad's plane."

Will shook his head in dismissal. "Nothing to be scared of, dude. We'll all go." He smiled at Evie and said, "I'll be your personal skiing tutor."

We walked home in silence. I wasn't purposely trying to not talk, but my mind was such a jumble that I was too busy trying to sort out my thoughts.

Mostly, I felt stupid. There was a small part of me that had started thinking that maybe Will Parker was enjoying fake-dating me.

But after the night at the diner, watching him grin and fawn and chat Evie up, I realized that the whole time he was being so helpful and sweet with me trying to get back at Jake, he was just trying to get to Evie!

And I mean, why wouldn't he? Evie was gorgeous. She was prettier than Sabrina, and her personality was much easier to take, if you liked the cheery-student-council-president-joins-every-club-there-is type.

The truth was that Will Parker liked every and all types of girls. And every and all types of girls liked him. Of course Evie shouldn't be any different.

"Hey, why are you so quiet?"

"Huh?" I looked up and noticed that Will was standing three feet behind me. "What are you doing?"

"Waiting for you to notice that I stopped walking."

"Oh, sorry. I was thinking."

"Okay." He moved to catch up to where I was standing. "Tell me."

"Nothing."

"Come on. Aren't you happy? I thought that went really well."

"But that was only because you kept talking to Evie the whole night!" I spat.

Will stopped walking again. "Wasn't that the plan?"

I shook my head and crossed my arms. "No."

"Yes it was," he said, confused.

"Fine. You're right."

"Why are you so cranky? I thought we got what you wanted. Now you're going to take this awesome trip with Jake, and it was all my doing." Will smiled at me, like he'd done me this big favor. "You know what? You're welcome."

I shook my head again, and said, "That was supposed to be *our* trip."

He raised an eyebrow, and my face started getting red again. I sounded like a jealous girl. "I thought you would like this better." From his voice and the way his face looked, I could tell that he was being completely honest.

I immediately felt sorry. I didn't know why I was behaving like this, like a spoiled brat who wanted all the boys in town just for herself. "I'm sorry, Will," I said.

His face softened and the curves of his mouth tilted up. "Okay."

"I just didn't know that you liked Evie." And then I began to walk. He ran to catch up to me but didn't say anything the rest of the walk home.

The moon was full, and so the woods and snow were glistening. There was as much light reflecting as there ever was these days, even in daytime. The only sound was the crunch of our feet over the snow. I could hear him breathing, and I could see the stream of our breath greeting the night air. I shoved my hands in my pockets. He did the same.

When we got to my house, a lot of the lights were on, and I could see that my brother was playing video games with my dad.

We walked to the front door. I turned to Will and said, "Do you want to come in and play with Brian?"

He laughed. "Nah. I should hang out with kids my own age."

I laughed and looked at my toes. "Will, I'm sorry."

"Don't worry." He wasn't smiling anymore.

"Thank you," I said quietly.

"Jessie, just so you know, I don't like Evie," he said.

Then he stepped in closer to me, put a hand on my waist and another on my shoulder, and kissed me. Right there on my doorstep! And the awful thing was that I kissed him back, without a second thought. I wrapped my arms around his neck and we kept kissing, until I could hear my father rapping on the inside of the front door.

I was mortified.

Will drew back, shoved his hands in his pockets, and said, "See you around, Jessie."

He hadn't called me Whitman the entire night.

Chapter 13

"*H*e what!" Abby screeched so loudly I expected the ice to shatter.

The girls and I were skating in the enclosed outdoor rink at the resort. The rink was usually crowded with figure skaters and junior hockey teams from all around the area. Today the rink had free skate hours, so I brought Brian and Tiffany to skate while I filled the girls in and waited for their reaction.

Abby was clearly shocked. In fact, she, who even in the best of times could barely keep her balance, tripped over her toe pick and went careening into Erin.

Erin, an out-of-place, black-clothed black-berry on hockey skates, caught Abby. The two of them slipped about a yard from me. They were holding on to each other for dear life and staring at me like two uncoordinated deer trapped in the path of oncoming traffic. I pushed off and skated for them. I pried them apart, holding Abby up with my left hand and Erin up with my right.

"You guys are worse than Brian," I said as the person mentioned caught sight of us and began skating headlong in our direction. "Don't you dare!" I shouted at him, but it was too late. Brian's favorite thing to do on skates was to gather as much speed as possible, then stop right in front of me, spraying me with a sheet of upward flying ice.

"God, I hate your little brother," Erin grumbled, patting at her black shirt and pants. Brian skated away, guffawing in delight.

Abby clutched my one arm with both hands, and I let go of Erin to give her my full balance. We began to skate, me moving backward and her moving forward, like a pair of ballroom dancers. I had no idea how my friend could be so bad at outdoor activities. It wasn't like there were a lot of other things to do here.

Once she had her balance, she said, "Um, can we go back to the part where you said that

Will Parker kissed you?" She squeaked again and nearly pulled me down with her.

"Okay, Michelle Kwan, let's go sit if we're going to talk," Erin said, and I heartily agreed. I flashed her a look of gratitude. Abby was little but kind of heavy when she was on skates and in a parka.

We skated over to the side of the rink, stepped through the door in the boards, and made our way to the Choco Shack, a little brick hut where you could order hot beverages and snacks. We each ordered a hot chocolate, then went to sit on one of the hockey benches. You weren't technically allowed to sit there unless you were a member of a participating hockey team, but Erin hated that rule and made it her cause to break it whenever we were skating.

I caught Brian's eye to let him know where we were, and he responded by setting us in his sights and coming at us like a kamikaze pilot. Once we were all sprayed, and Brian was skating away gleefully, Abby and Erin turned to me. I was conveniently seated in the middle.

"He kissed you?!" Abby shrieked. Poor girl had been holding it in for too long.

Erin started laughing and held her hot chocolate in front of her nose. "Please tell me that Sabrina saw this kiss."

"No, she didn't. It was later. When he walked me home."

This got their attention. Their looks, which were on me to begin with, became more intense. In fact, they each leaned in and asked at the same time, "What?"

Then Erin went on, "You mean, this was a for-real kiss?"

"Oh my GOD!" Abby couldn't help herself.

"Shush. Come on. What if one of his friends is here?" I pleaded.

Erin gestured with her hand, sweeping across the entire rink. "Where? Where would his friends be?"

"I don't know. I'm sorry. I'm just . . . I'm confused."

Erin nodded her head, agreeing that I was confused. "Start from the beginning."

Abby couldn't wait for that, though. "Was he a good kisser?"

"Yes!" This word tumbled out of me, like I couldn't wait to confess. "Really good. Different from Jake. Like, I think he's kissed a lot of girls, you guys."

Abby bit her lip. Erin continued her professorial-like nodding. "Tell us what happened," she said.

"Okay." I raised the hot chocolate to my face, so that it could be warmed by the steam. "He picked me up. We laid out the ground rules, you know, that the whole date was to help me win Jake back. We went to the diner. The four of us talked. And the whole time, I thought that Will kind of liked Evie. He invited her to go skiing with us up to Grizzly."

"Really? I thought he was planning that for you two," Abby said pensively.

Erin answered before I could. "He was definitely planning it for the two of you."

I looked at her. "How do you know that?"

"He told me," Erin said calmly as if this were the most normal thing in the world.

"When did he tell you?" I asked.

She sipped her hot chocolate, all nonchalance. "When we were playing video games yesterday."

"What did he say?" Abby and I asked the question together.

"Nothing. Just, he said he asked you to go to Grizzly Mountain with him."

"Like a date? A real date?" Abby asked. I waited for Erin to answer. Now my cheeks felt so warm I didn't need the hot chocolate.

"I think so." Erin leaned in. "He made me promise not to say anything so you can't tell him that I told you."

"That's complicated," Abby said.

"I know," Erin concurred.

"I don't understand," I exclaimed.

Erin put down her hot chocolate. "I think he likes you. Like, likes you likes you."

"Did he say that?" I asked.

"No, but he doesn't have to. I can tell."

My guts were churning. To think that I'd felt a little jealous when I'd seen them playing video games. I shook my head. "I don't understand."

"What's to understand? You are always

going on and on about how I should go out with him. You should listen to your reasons and go out with him yourself."

Abby touched my hand. "Jess?"

"I don't get it. If he wanted to go on a date with me, and went so far as to ask my dad to fly us all the way to Grizzly Mountain, why'd he invite Evie and Jake to come?"

Erin's face scrunched up. "Yeah, that's something to figure out, I guess."

"When exactly did he invite them?" Abby asked, as confused-sounding as I felt.

"During dinner, he and Evie were talking the whole time, and he seemed to really like her! You know that tone he uses with Mrs. Mulch in English, when he hasn't read the assignment?"

"Yeah?" the two of them said in unison.

"It was that tone."

"Hmmm," Erin said, her face solemnly in concentration. "Weird."

"But he kissed you, right?" Abby asked.

"Yeah. After he said he didn't like Evie."

"But he invited her to Grizzly Mountain."

"Where he's going to spend the whole day with her, teaching her to ski."

Erin shook her head. "I'm working tonight. I'll see if I can get the truth out of him."

Abby agreed. "That's a good idea."

I exhaled. I didn't understand boys at all.

After Brian finished skating, I brought him home and then went to work my shift at Snow Cones. I felt cranky and irritable and needed to soothe my feelings with ice cream.

When I got there, my mother was behind the counter, and so I offered to go back to the kitchen and work on the ice-cream flavors for the next day.

Standing with my hair tied in a ponytail and an apron around my waist, I measured out eggs, cream, and sugar. I picked out the special ingredients, like the peppermint, the green tea, and the licorice. I shredded chocolate and measured walnuts, raisins, and butterscotch chips.

And all the while I tried to sort out why my insides felt so scrambled.

The best thing to do was a wholesale review.

My entire life had been upended by Jake deciding that he didn't want to be my boyfriend anymore and then not even telling me about it. But in the past two days or so, I started to think that maybe I didn't want to be his girlfriend. I didn't know when the tables had been turned.

I had a whole plan with Jake! We were going to travel together, and then go to UAA together. I was going to study geology, and he was going to study law. We'd spend the summer break in the States, or abroad even, and the winter break here, where winter break was best.

And now, here I was getting ready to go on a day trip with him, and all I could think about was Will.

Will Parker, the boy in our class who everyone liked. The boy who the teachers loved. The boy from ESPN. The boy who promised to win an Olympic gold medal for our town. The boy who had rescued me from a post-Brian collision and walked me to my mom. A boy who pretended to be my boyfriend. A boy who kissed me.

When I had been Jake's girlfriend, I never felt this confused. He never made my stomach feel like it was trapped in a blender. He was honest and didn't play games. Except for this whole breakup thing.

I plopped the batch of vanilla into the large metallic tub my mother used for ice-cream making. I crammed it into the freezer and repeated this task until I had made twenty tubs.

By the time my mother drove me home, I had decided. All that was happening was that I was falling under Will's weirdo hypnotic spell that he cast on everyone. He probably didn't think about me at all! I suddenly felt bad for Sabrina, and the blond girl at the lodge, and Mrs. Mulch, and all the other women of Willow Hill who had confused Will's charming personality for actual interest.

My mind was made up. I was going to take the opportunity that Will had given me, and I was going to once and for all tell Jake that I wanted to be his girlfriend again, his *only* girlfriend. Even if he had trouble deciding, after one day with Will, Evie wouldn't even know Jake's name anymore. She'd feel the way I did now, all jittery and crushy on him. Well, I wasn't going to let this continue. Will Parker had me all confused and I wanted it to end. I knew what I wanted: I wanted to go to UAA with Jake, and to be done with the stomach mambo.

Chapter 14

Jake looked green in the plane.

My father, who always got a kick out of passengers who had flight sickness, dipped and curved among the mountaintops. Part of this was because my father loved nothing more than showing off the Alaskan scenery, but I suspected that part of the aerial theatrics had to do with highlighting Jake's "softness."

I hadn't seen Will since the night of our double date. And when he met us at the airport that morning, he acted as if nothing had taken place between us at all. He smiled at me in a friendly way and then climbed into the plane and sat down right next to Evie. His cool demeanor was fine by me. I was bound and determined to not be just another dumb Willow Hill girl with an unrequited crush on the boy nobody could have. Will probably kissed a different girl every night and then couldn't tell you who it had been the next morning.

I sat down next to Jake and concentrated on helping him through his air sickness. I fed him crackers and held a bottle of water for him. At one point, Jake rested his eyes and I took the opportunity to spy on Will and Evie. Part of my developing Will-sickness was that I couldn't stop noticing how good he looked, all the time. He wore his favorite navy snow pants plus a fleece pullover and a navy parka. I tried to distract myself by staring at Evie, who also looked spectacular. Her hair was blond and shiny. Her lips were covered in sparkly lip gloss and her cheeks were dusky rose. I thought how lucky I was that Will was working for me and not against me. Without an uneven playing surface, Green Jake would definitely pick her over me.

By the time my father landed the plane, it was nearly ten o'clock and the sun was just starting to peek out over the mountaintops of the Grizzly area.

I'd never been there, ever, but my father

had spoken of this place enough that I knew this would be an extraordinary day. Grizzly was north of where I lived, and it was a little bit *more* of everything than Willow Hill: more cold, more mountains, more snow. When my feet touched the ground, a wind wrapped around my face and nearly knocked me back. All my boy troubles were momentarily forgotten. I stretched my arms to the sky.

"This is going to be a good day!" I pronounced to nobody in general.

But Evie took up the rallying cry. She also spread out her arms to the sky. "I feel it too!"

"Okay, kids, I'll be back for you at the end of the day. Meet me back here sharply at six o'clock. Got it?" My father looked at me, and pressed a fifty-dollar bill into my hands.

He pointed toward the front of the airplane hangar. Waiting there was an old school bus that had been painted over with blue paint and transformed into a shuttle for the ski area. I hugged my father good-bye and then the four of us marched over to the bus. I was preparing to do whatever I had to in order to sit next to Jake, but Will grabbed my hand and pulled me into a seat right next to him. My stomach turned, my annoyance level rose, and I was forced to watch Evie and Jake sit next to each other a few rows behind us.

Will leaned close to me and smiled. "Are you ready?"

He was close enough to kiss. I turned my head and chanted to myself, *I will not be a dumb Willow Hill girl* three times. I forced myself to think of our walk home and how Will had probably forgotten it already. I looked to the aisle of the bus before returning my gaze directly ahead of me.

"As I'll ever be," I responded without making eye contact.

"Good." He slid down and raised one knee, resting it against the seat in front of us. I tried not to stare at his ankle, which was visible as his white sock had slipped to the edge of his sneaker. "You okay?"

"Hmm-mmm." I looked behind us, to see what Jake and Evie were up to. Apparently bus rides made him as sick as airplane rides. He was doubled over and she was rubbing his back.

"You're gonna love it here, Whitman," Will said.

"I hear the powder's good."

"Yeah." He poked me in the ribs, and my stomach leaped. "Listen, I know you're going to be *busy* and all, but after we ski, I want to take you somewhere."

"You do?"

He smiled wide and I chanted to myself again. "I don't know," I said finally.

"Jessie," he said in a low voice. "There's an animal sanctuary."

I couldn't help myself. "There are animals?"

"Yes. After you're done with that green kid"—he motioned behind us—"I want an hour of your time. There's a Nature Loop. You can hike it up to an animal enclosure. There're deer, elk, moose. I saw a bear there once."

I couldn't answer. An hour was all he'd need to make me fall completely head over heels with him. There was no way I could go, even if part of me really, really wanted to.

He poked me in the ribs again and grinned.

"It's romantic. You'll like it."

There wasn't a trace of anything mean or nasty in his face. In fact, he looked completely earnest.

He was driving me crazy.

I swallowed hard and tried to change the subject. "Do you think you can teach her how to ski?"

He looked at me like I'd asked the stupidest question ever.

"I can teach anybody to ski."

"Well, not anybody," I joked.

"Yeah, not Erin."

We laughed, and I thought to myself how long ago it seemed that I wanted to set him up with Erin. Now I couldn't imagine him with any other girl. Which of course wasn't very fair of me.

We got silent again, and the bus rattled on.

"How much longer?" I asked.

"Half hour or so."

I wanted to scream. I didn't think I could take another half hour of this ride, especially with the long silences. The knee that wasn't pressed into the back of the seat in front of us was pressed into mine, and my stomach had gone from nervousness to outright nausea. I was so uncomfortable that I blurted:

"You know, I wanted to fix you up with Erin."

"Clark?"

"Yeah."

"Nah. I don't think she'd like me that way."

This got my attention. I had to assume that he assumed he could get any girl he wanted.

"And anyway, she's like my sister or something."

He caught my eye then and I couldn't help but smile at him just a bit.

Finally after what seemed like an eternity, the bus pulled into a big parking lot, and the bus driver opened the door. Evie helped Jake to his feet and they made their way off the bus.

Just before we stood to join them outside, Will said, "Besides, you're the only girl for me." And then he kissed me again, on the cheek. It was quick, but he had unmistakably put his lips near mine, and for a moment I thought it might not be so bad to be one of the pining Willow Hill girls.

The minute we descended from the bus, Will took over. He told us that he'd take Evie to the bunny hill, where he would allegedly work all kinds of skier magic on her. She looked thrilled and whether she was excited by the prospect of finally learning to ski or of being with Will, I didn't know. Then he reminded me about the Nature Loop, the path to the animal sanctuary he'd told me about on the bus. There was no hint that he had meant anything by what he had said about me being the only girl for him. Will was the king of mixed messages. Though if I thought about it, maybe I was the queen of mixed messages, because I *was* letting Will steal kisses even though I was there to be getting back Jake's love.

"Okay, so we'll meet back here at five fifteen?" Will asked.

"But what about lunch?" Jake asked.

"I won't want to stop for lunch," I said. Who cared about lunch when we were here in this beautiful country?

"That's my girl." Will smiled at me. Again, an annoying little jolt went through my stomach. "'Kay, Evie. Ready for your world to be rocked?"

Now it was Evie's turn to giggle. "I'm ready."

"'Kay. We'll see you here at five fifteen." Then he leaned forward and whispered in my ear, "Meet me here an hour before that." Then he kissed me on the cheek AGAIN. Right in front of everybody. He was getting carried away and he knew it. Before he pulled away from me, he gave me an evil grin. I knew then, in that second, that he was totally toying with me.

They disappeared from view, into the large red stone lodge in front of us. I turned to Jake; it was just him and me now. I took a deep breath and could feel my insides return to normal.

"Feeling okay?" I asked.

Jake's face turned as red as it had been green before. "I'm a baby. I'm sorry."

"It's okay," I said. Something about how he said that, so vulnerable and without any thought of game-playing, made me smile. Life as Jake's real girlfriend had been much easier on my stomach than life as Will's fake girlfriend.

"You want to ski with me?" I asked.

He reached for my skis and hoisted them up with his own. "Of course I do."

Jake and I had a great time.

First, we went into the lodge and paid for our passes. Before we hit the slopes, I bought us each a granola bar and a bottle of water. He was grateful and gave me one of those toe-curling smiles that had won my heart in the first place. I thought to myself that when he smiled, you knew he meant it. Not like Will, whose smile gave you the feeling that he had an ulterior motive.

Then Jake and I skied, and the whole time he was chatty and friendly and calm, and I started to feel comfortable and happy. I barely thought about Will at all, and when I did, I chanted my favorite mantra and vowed to forget him.

We raced, running the course so many times that we lost track of who was winning. The only less-than-perfect moment was when he said that he wanted to check on Evie. We trudged our way over to the bunny hill, but she wasn't there and neither was Will. I wondered where they had wandered off to, but Jake found them.

They were on the beginner's hill, a hill that in any other resort would have been an intermediate. We were in the north. The mountains were bigger here. The slopes were harder to navigate, their angles were more severe. The first thing I saw was the blue burst of Will on a pair of skis. It struck me that I'd never seen him ski much. He always snowboarded, but here he was careening down the mountain with as much grace as an Olympian.

The real magic was that behind him was Evie, and she was skiing like an old pro.

"I can't believe it!" Jake exclaimed.

"Me neither!" I was shocked. Will had come through.

"Your boyfriend is a magician."

"What?" I turned to Jake, not sure what he meant at first.

"I didn't think anyone could teach her to ski."

"Oh. Yeah. Will's something else."

We tried to catch up with them, but they were too far away, and I had the feeling that if we connected with them, then my time with Jake would be done. And I wasn't ready for that yet.

So I persuaded him to run the big hill with me again, which he did.

At the bottom, we took another break. We found a little restaurant in the main lodge and I bought the two of us roast beef sandwiches.

We sat across from each other at large picnic tables and ate in comfortable silence. My stomach was completely at ease. *This*, I thought to myself, *is what a relationship should be. Two people who can have pleasant days together without nausea.*

"Jake."

He looked up at me. His hair was messy from the hat he'd been wearing, and his skin was still red from the wind.

"I'm having a really good time."

He smiled. "Me too."

I bit my lip. "Listen, Will told me about this animal sanctuary. You wanna go with me?"

He ripped the remains of his bread into a

dozen tiny pieces. "What about, you know, Will?"

"He won't mind," I said quickly. And though for a moment I questioned whether that was true, I stood, determined to put this whole Will thing behind me. If that meant ditching him, well then, I could live with that. Honestly, he probably wouldn't care.

Jake stood too. We smiled at each other, then stashed our skis behind a counter at the lodge and took the chairlift up to the trail leading to the Nature Loop.

"It's colder up here, huh?" he asked, walking beside me. We'd been walking for what seemed like an hour, and there was no sign of any animals. I chalked that up to my terrible sense of direction.

"Freezing," I said, looking around the path for any sight of a deer or an elk. I would've been happy to see a squirrel at that point.

"I can't ever imagine that it can be colder than it gets down in Juneau, and then in Willow Hill, forget it. But here, God. The reindeer must freeze their antlers off."

I looked at him sideways. "The reindeer must freeze their antlers off?"

He smiled. "What? I'm trying to be funny."

"Keep trying," I joked.

He gave me a playful shove in the arm. "Hey!" I shouted in mock anger. "That's it."

And, in classic Brian Whitman fashion, I scooped up a handful of wet, icy snow and pelted him with it.

"Aw, you're dead!" He scrambled off the path and began scooping up his own fistfuls of snow. I headed in the opposite direction, where there was a dense stand of pine trees. I had learned my lessons well: You needed cover to avoid excess hits.

I peeked from behind a pine tree long enough to vault another snowball over the path toward Jake. I had thrown it so terribly, it hit the ground six feet in front of him.

"You throw like a girl!" he called out.

"I *am* a girl!" I defended myself. Then I leaned down to scoop up another snowball, and waited until I saw him reaching down to do the same before leaving my hiding place, running up to the edge of the walking path, and nailing him on the back of the neck with an icy bullet.

"Ouch!" He reached his hand back to touch his neck, which was now red and covered in moisture. "You're dead!" He ran after me and tackled me to the ground just as we reached the edge of the trees, but I was a slippery one. I slipped out from his grasp and made a run for it. I ran past three, four, five, six trees before stopping to catch my breath behind a wide, round, knobby birch.

I was breathing hard, and so enjoying myself that I wasn't even thinking. I bent low to craft together another missile, and while I did, I looked out for him. I had gone too far into the forest. It was so thick with trees and blowing wind, I could hardly see anything.

I took a step or two forward. Nothing. I thought he must be hiding behind a tree, waiting for me to come closer, but I wasn't going to fall for that one.

So I turned around. "ARGGHHHHH!"

I screamed in scared delight, just as he

pelted me right in the chest. He had been standing directly behind me, quiet as a mouse, waiting to nail me.

"Got ya!" he shouted, and then collapsed
onto the floor of the woods with me. I was
laughing so hard from being scared, I couldn't
catch my breath. "You didn't hear me at all?"
He was laughing and smiling, clearly pleased
with himself.

"You should be a spy! You're stealthy like
a cat!"

He was leaning against the base of the birch
tree, the one that had been my temporary shelter. I started to laugh again, and laid back into
the snow to catch my breath, and stare up into
the sky.

"Hey! Look!" I pointed upward. "Northern
lights."

"Oh! Cool!" He laid down right beside me,
and we stared up into the sky. The lights were
streaking across in lines of green, red, orange,
and blue.

"They haven't been visible from the Hill," I
said quietly.

"Why are you whispering?" He laughed.

I laughed too. "I didn't want to disturb the lights."

We turned to look at each other. "You're such a weird girl."

"Ssshhh. Look at the lights." And then we did. We laid back in the snow, and despite the cold and the wind and the wet, we stared at the northern lights dancing in the sky. I hadn't seen them since the beginning of school, and I didn't want anything to disrupt the show.

After a while of watching the streaks of starlit gases fill the sky, Jake whispered, "Do you remember the first summer we met?"

I smiled to myself. "Yeah. I do."

He was talking about that first time we watched the lights together. We'd met the week before, in ski class. The first night I ate dinner at his house, we sat on the deck of his family's cabin and watched the northern lights. He had never seen them before and at first was a little scared. When I got home that night, I knew that I had fallen in love for the first time.

I turned to look at him again, and found that he wasn't looking at the lights, he was looking at me. He reached for me and pulled himself closer, and then he held my hand, right under the northern lights and the pine trees and probably the snowy owls.

He held up our hands. "Okay?"

"That's okay," I whispered. We stayed like that, and then something started buzzing around in my head, an internal, Whitman alarm bell.

"Holy crow!" I said, pushing him from me. "What time is it?"

He sat up and pulled his cell phone from his pocket. "No service. I don't know."

"Oh no." I didn't have to check. I knew that it was way late, and that we'd never make it to my father's meeting point by six o'clock.

I reached into my pocket. Of course, I knew my cell phone wouldn't work. But I kept a small pocket watch, something my father told me to always have on me. He took great pride in raising me and Brian so that we knew how to survive, and the pocket watch, along with a compass, and always having granola bars, was part of that education.

I finally found the watch at the bottom of my pack.

"Oh no," I said, terrified.

"What?" Jake asked.

"It's five forty-five. My father is going to kill me. And you."

Chapter 15

I was dead meat.

Not only were Jake and I late, but we were lost. It took us about a half hour to relocate the path. It turned out that in the midst of snow and wind, snowy paths were easily blown away.

Jake, while we were searching, was calm and collected but definitely not understanding the problem. And the problem was, in a word, Dad. He couldn't just take off whenever he wanted. He'd probably get snowbound, and who knows how long we'd have to stay up here.

And though ninety percent of me was worried about losing my life, the other ten percent was basking in the glow of the fact that Jake held my hand while we ran down the path. Well, nine and a half percent. The other half percent kept thinking about Will, about how he had asked for one hour of my time so that he could take me to the animal sanctuary. About how ditching him was probably the meanest thing I'd ever done to anybody. If I'd have kept my promise, I probably wouldn't be lost like this.

I shook my head to dismiss that half percent. I squeezed Jake's hand and reminded myself that I was thrilled. We'd gotten lost, but found each other here in the snowy woods! This would be a comforting thought in my final moments as my father was literally taking my life.

Then, as Jake and I were beneath a large tree, frantically turning in circles, trying to find the right way out, I heard a voice.

"Whitman?! Whitman?! Jessie?!"

I released Jake's hand and went running. "Will! Will!" By this time, there was no light except starlight, and Will's suit was dark so it was hard to make him out. He was no dummy, though. He carried a flashlight and was waving it back and forth.

"I see you!" I shouted, and went running toward the little light.

When he made me out, he ran. When we reached each other, he put his arms around me and buried his face in my neck. "You found me!" I half shouted, half murmured into his hair.

"Sure thing. Were you trying to get to the Nature Loop?"

I took a huge step backward, to where Jake had come up behind me. "Jake and I tried to find it." Even in the dark, I could see Will take the two of us in. He searched my face and I found myself averting his gaze at first. But then I met his eyes and smiled, to let him know that my get-Jake-back plan was working. He smiled back, but it wasn't as full as it could've been. It didn't reach his eyes. I wondered if he'd been kissing Evie while Jake and I had been having a stupid snowball fight.

"Your dad's here," he said finally.

I tilted my head back to look at the stars. "I'll miss you, northern lights," I said aloud.

"You ain't kidding. Your dad's one scary dude." Will reached for my pack. "Come on, I can get us back." He lifted my pack onto his back, catching my eye as he did so. While his back was turned, Jake grabbed my gloved hand and squeezed it.

❊ ❊ ❊

When we reached the lodge, my father was still searching for me. It was another hour before he came back, and when he saw me sitting in the lodge, sipping hot chocolate as if nothing had happened, he lifted me off the ground in a giant bear hug. Then he slammed me down like an insect under a shoe and gritted his teeth.

"Your mother is going to kill us," he said.

Jake tried to keep out of his sight, which I thought was smart thinking on his part.

We were stranded at Grizzly Mountain for the night. My father, after calling my mother and instructing her to call Evie's, Jake's, and Will's parents, booked two rooms in the local motel near the airstrip, one for me and Evie and one for Will and Jake. He warned that we'd have a forty-five-minute warning before we had to dash to the airport, so we were supposed to get as much sleep as we could. He slept at the airport hangar.

I was exhausted and dirty and starving. Evie stretched my wet clothes across the heating unit in our hotel room while I took a shower.

"They should be dry soon. Your socks are already done." Evie threw the rolled-up spool of socks at me as I exited the bathroom, and I caught them one-handed.

She sat on the double bed farthest from where I stood, the one near the windows. Her legs were stretched out in front of her and she was rubbing lotion into her toes. "I know, I know. I'm about to shower. But they're so sore."

"Blisters?" I asked, sitting on the bed. I wanted to keep the small talk going. I didn't know if she was angry at me, or what. I had gotten lost on a mountain with her boyfriend.

"Yeah. I didn't feel them until I took off the ski boots."

"That means you had a good day on the slopes," I responded.

She pulled the long blond hair from her face and wrapped it into a ball, which she tied into a bun without using a ponytail holder.

"We were worried."

"I'm really sorry. I got us lost."

Her head tilted. I thought she was going to say something, but instead she stood and walked into the bathroom.

While she was in the shower, I put on my half wet clothes and wandered down to the motel lobby. There was a little restaurant that made burgers and things, and my father had given me money with strict orders to buy everyone dinner. I let Evie know to meet me there.

The boys weren't there yet, which was good because I needed time to think. I wished that Abby and Erin were with me. I needed their advice. I didn't know what I wanted anymore. I mean, I did know, I wanted Jake and I wanted to not want Will. But I hadn't bargained on the Evie factor, and that factor was this: I didn't want her to feel as sad as I had felt when Jake broke up with me for her. And judging by how Jake had held my hand all afternoon, that's precisely what was in store for her.

Erin would say that you shouldn't want a boyfriend who was capable of holding hands with another girl. And Abby would say that I should follow my heart. My mother would tell me to forget boys and concentrate on getting into a good college.

None of this advice helped me feel better for doing what girls like Sabrina did, stealing another girl's boyfriend.

I ordered a Coke and stirred the straw

around and around the ice, while my mind furiously worked through my options.

And then all three of them showed up at once. Jake had changed into a pair of jeans and his cheeks were rosy from the day spent outside. He smiled when he saw me, even though Evie was walking with him and whispering in his ear. I gulped down the rest of my Coke to drown the miserable feelings I had about myself.

Will walked past the two of them, with a purpose. He got to the booth I had chosen and slid in beside me.

"You okay?" he asked, and dropped his head on my shoulder.

"What are you doing?" I shook him off.

"We're boyfriend and girlfriend, remember?" Will said, drawing my face to meet his eye.

"Right. Right," I said, the feeling that I was a terrible person deepening.

"I'm a good boyfriend," Will said before turning to the others, who were sliding into the booth.

We ordered four burgers, and Will told us how he transformed Evie from an ugly non-skiing duckling into a beautiful, racing-down-the-intermediate-hills swan. Evie glowed with pride. Jake didn't say much and spent most of the meal looking right at me. Evie had to prompt him to pay attention. I found myself getting a little bit mad at him. How dare he stare at me right in front of his new girlfriend? Didn't he care about her feelings at all?

After we were done with the burgers, the waitress brought us all ice-cream sundaes. Jake got up to go to the bathroom, and Evie followed.

"Looks like your master plan is working," Will said, popping a cherry into his mouth.

"Yeah," I grumbled into my lap.

Will sighed and rolled the cherry stem beneath his palm, back and forth, back and forth.

I thought of cool things to say. Sabrina would probably be loud and flirty and fearless, being in the driver's seat of her love triangle. I was sitting in the backseat of mine. In fact, I felt at the moment that I was stuffed in the trunk of my own love triangle, unable to breathe.

"Are you just not going to talk? What, are you done with me now?" He was tying the cherry stem into knots.

I crossed my arms and tried not to look at him.

Will tilted his head and dropped a hand onto my knee. My face started to flush.

"You have to stop," I said, half to my lap and half to him. "It's not funny."

Will removed his hand and nodded twice. "Sure thing, Whitman. I get it." Then mercifully, Evie arrived back at our table. I was never so happy to see a girlfriend of Jake's who wasn't me in my whole life.

Chapter 16

The good thing about being in mortal trouble with my parents was that it made me forget my confusing love life.

My father barely spoke to me while we were in the plane, but I did notice that he kept a close eye on the proximity of both boys to me. He made me sit next to him in the cockpit and barked out orders to the three of them whenever they started to relax. By the time we landed and drove back to Willow Hill, I could tell that Evie, Jake, and especially Will were terrified. I'd never seen Will so polite to an adult before, saying sir and please and thank you after every comment.

I sat in the passenger seat of my dad's truck and when we pulled into the resort's parking lot, the three of them leaped out of the back.

Will pulled Evie's bag out of the cab for her, and she waved at me with a wistful expression on her face before turning for her cabin. She probably thought she'd never see me again, because she probably thought that my father was going to murder me. She was probably right.

Jake sauntered after her and when he caught up to her, they turned together to walk home. Will, who I could see in the passenger-side mirror, leaned against the front window of the resort entrance. His bags were on the ground, and until Cam and Jay surprised him by jumping on his back simultaneously, he stared at the truck.

All of these things were forgotten the minute my dad turned onto the main road.

I decided to head the angry father routine off at the pass. "How angry are you?"

My father kept his eyes on the road. "I don't know yet. Wait until we get home. Your mother will have something to say."

"Daddy, you don't know how mad you are?"

"Nope. Not until your mother tells me."

I shook my head. "Well, I'm sorry."

"I know you are, pumpkin." He patted my head. "I was just worried about takeoff. I knew you weren't up to no good."

"Thanks, Dad."

"But if I'm wrong, then you have to forget this conversation. Deal?"

"Deal."

My father is six foot five, but I have never once felt the kind of fear of him that I do of my mother, who isn't much taller than five feet. When we pulled into our driveway, she was standing on the front stoop with her arms crossed over her chest. My brother, Brian, was leaning out the second-story window. Tiffany was with him. She was trying to hold his legs so that he could lean farther out the window to hear the punishment.

We got out of the truck, and my father walked forward. "Hey, honey," he said to my mother, sweeping her up for a kiss on the cheek. He always lifted her up to his level, sometimes just to have a conversation. As I moved toward the door, knowing that I'd have to pass her to get inside, I could hear him say, "Go easy. She feels bad enough."

When I stood in front of my mother, my father conveniently walked inside the house, though he lingered by the screen door. He pumped his fist at me, a signal that I should be strong.

Before I could say anything, Brian let out a squeal that sounded like a cat in the middle of a nighttime fight. "Eeeeeeyyyy-yyyyyyyyyowwwwwwww! You're scratch-ing me!"

Without even taking her eyes from me, she shouted, "Brian Bartholomew Whitman, if you fall out of that window I am going to kill you!"

"I'm not doing anything!" he countered, before saying in a strangled, quieter voice to Tiffany, "Bring me in! Bring me in!"

I shot him a death glare but recognized my opportunity and attempted to go around my mother.

Her arm shot out and reeled me in. She looked up at me, her hands gripping my arms.

"Mom, I just lost track of time. I'm really sorry."

She pursed her lips and assessed me. If she were reading my mind, I hoped that she'd have the good sense to skip to the ending. "Go wash up. We're having a family lunch."

As far as punishments went, family lunches were manageable. Even if they included Brian.

My mother kept her temper in check, and other than telling me that I couldn't go to Anchorage that night to go shopping with Erin and Abby, there didn't seem to be much of a punishment in sight. So I spent most of the day playing video games with Brian and Tiffany.

"You have to shoot that guy or he's going to—I told you. Now you're dead. I told you," Brian said to Tiffany, who was on her knees on our love seat, her hair flying around in all sorts of directions, her cheeks red, and her face screwed up in a ball of concentration.

"That's not how I do it!"

"That's why you're dead."

"You're the one who's dead!" And she let fly

a karate chop with her left leg that nearly took my brother's head off.

This, as I had ascertained from my day with them, was how they communicated. They fought and then lashed out and then quieted down and then fought some more. The two of them seemed to be blissfully enjoying themselves. I sank down into the couch cushions. "Let me play. It's my turn."

"Jessie, you can play after Tiffany's dead."

"She just died!"

"Jessie, I'll tell you when," Brian stated matter-of-factly.

My brother was chivalrous, and it burned me up to be witnessing how easy it was for these two to get along. When did it get so complicated? I guessed that sometime between sixth grade and junior year, the whole balance of the world became topsy-turvy on its axis. I wished for the simpler days when karate-chopping a boy in the head let him know that he was yours forever.

"Okay. Your turn." Tiffany threw her controller at me. It landed on my lap. I handed it back to her.

"You can go."

She eyed me suspiciously.

"Take it!" Brian commanded. "Before she changes her mind."

"Give me *your* turn," I spat.

He pulled the controller to his chest and turned his body, as if he were protecting it from me. "No way."

Tiffany kicked him again. "You have to share!"

"Hey!" I reached out to keep her from landing another foot on my brother's arm. But the two of them pushed me away and started laughing.

I couldn't take the tween-love show anymore, so I wandered into the kitchen. I stared out the back doors, at the snow. The deer with her baby was grazing again. When they ambled out of our yard, I let myself out onto the back porch.

I sat on one of our deck chairs, pulling up my knees for warmth. I wondered where Will was, and then reminded myself that I should be

thinking about Jake, about what he was thinking about our time on the mountain. After five
minutes of this chilly self-reflection, I felt a
buzzing on my hip.

It was my cell phone, with a text.

WHERE R U?

From Jake. My fingers flew across the key-
board.

GROUNDED 4 NIGHT.

Two seconds later:

2 BAD. LOOK TO UR LEFT.

I did. And Jake was hiding in the trees in
my backyard, wearing the same thin coat he'd
worn that time I saw him on his porch, the time
when he ran from me.

He smiled and then punched something into
his cell phone.

SAFE TO SIT?

I looked up, grinned, and nodded.

He walked over to me, pulled a chair close,
and sat.

"Hey," I said.

"Hey," he responded.

"You in any trouble?" I asked.

"Nah. Your mom didn't tell anybody anything, just that the visibility was too bad for your dad to fly."

"Oh," I said, looking into my house involuntarily for my parents. They'd covered for us. "That was cool."

"Yep."

I refastened my arms around my legs.

Jake's foot tapped the floor.

I took a deep breath. I was not going to say anything. I repeated this in my head. I was not going to say anything.

He looked to me, then back into my house, and then at me. "Can we go in? I'm freezing."

"I'm not saying anything first," I responded.

He looked taken aback, and then when he regained his composure, he said, "Okay."

I raised my eyebrows at him.

He didn't say anything either. He slid my chair toward him. Then he reached out, held my hand, leaned in, and kissed me. It would've been an amazing moment, except for the screeching sound we heard coming from just behind us at the door.

"Jake Reid! I'm telling my sister!" Tiffany shouted while my brother held his sides to contain his laughter and pointed at us.

Chapter 17

It took a few days, but finally, my winter break was proceeding the way it was supposed to.

The morning after Tiffany shrieked into the night, I was in the middle of my normal angsty routine at Snow Cones with Erin and Abby when there arrived a dozen roses. Abby clapped her hands. Erin cast a doubtful eye over the entire scene.

They were from Jake, with a card that said that he had a lot to make up for.

Erin wanted to know what seventeen-year-old sent roses, but I ignored her.

We were officially back together that afternoon.

He broke up with Evie the way he should have broken up with me. Face-to-face, with no kissing and no mixed messages. This made me feel only slightly better, though when he told me that she was going back to Boise with her father early, I felt terrible all over again.

We returned to the way we'd been over the years. We spent our days skiing and our afternoons lingering at the Mountain Diner or some such place. We talked about taking a trip to Glacier National Park in the summer, we talked about going to college together, we talked about his father wanting to move to Willow Hill full-time.

The only difference was in me. I kept looking for Will, despite my best intentions to let my silly crush go. Each time I caught sight of him, he was either surrounded by a flock of blond freshmen or teaching out-of-towners the finer points of leaping into the air with your snowboard. The one time he caught my eye, he brought his finger to his brow in a salute.

"You can't just break up with him without saying anything!" Abby scolded me one morning while we were looking up Facebook pages in my room.

"I'm not dumping anybody! We weren't together!"

I hated when Abby thought ill of me, but she had every reason to. I was avoiding actually talking to Will because I wanted to pretend that I didn't care about him at all. If I talked to him, my stomach would flip and then I'd know I was lying to myself. But by not talking to him, I was essentially doing to him what Jake had done to me. Breakup by silent treatment.

Then there was the matter of the dance. Abby refused my requests to rent a tuxedo for Jake. She claimed she didn't have the time to take his measurements.

So the next day, I went to visit Erin at work.

"What's up?" she said, eating carrot sticks behind the counter. "You've got about five minutes before Mean Agnes shows up here with a broomstick, shooing you out."

"Is Will around?"

Erin's eyes widened. "I'll get him here." She whipped out her cell phone and texted him.

"What, he jumps when you call?"

"Something like that."

I grabbed a carrot stick and chewed it thoughtfully. "Erin, is Will like a brother to you?"

"Huh?"

"It's just, I don't understand why you don't want to date him."

Erin shrugged her shoulders. "It's like, I don't get that butterfly feeling when I look at him. You know?"

I looked at her. I did know.

Just then, Will bounded into the lodge. "Needed me, doll cakes?" he said to Erin before he spotted me. He slowed his steps and even looked like he was surprised to see me. The butterflies Erin had just mentioned were now flying around like caged birds in my stomach.

He looked good. His hair was sweaty and his face was red. I suddenly couldn't catch my breath.

Erin grimaced at him. "Not me. Her." She pointed at me, and then warned, "Take it outside.

I'm not filing any more of Agnes's stupid receipts from the 1980s."

"Okay, okay." Then he took my arm and tried to lead me out the door. "Ice cream on you?"

"Yeah, okay."

We walked to Snow Cones and he waited in a booth while I piled all his favorite flavors into the biggest dish I could find. When I put it in front of him, he ate half of it before saying anything. I was about to scream when he finally looked at me. "I haven't seen you around much."

"Yeah, I've been busy."

"I've noticed."

I didn't say anything.

"I was waiting for our fake breakup." He smiled at me and the butterflies started flying again.

"Will," I exhaled. He put his spoon down and looked at me. I noticed that his eyes were blue and quite serious. He was holding his breath too.

"Yeah?"

"Um. I know I haven't talked to you since the trip and all, but about the dance—"

"You're going with Jake, I know."

"No!"

He raised his eyebrows.

"Well, the tux is rented, and Abby altered it to fit you."

He blinked. "So you still want to go together?"

"Um. Yeah, if you don't mind."

He looked at me. "What about the guy?"

"He understands. He's not going now, because he broke up with Evie and everything."

"Hmmm."

"Listen, I know I've asked so much of you this break—"

"It's this important for you girls to show up Sabrina?"

My mouth fell open. "How'd you know?"

"Please. It's not really a secret how much you three hate her."

I bit my lip. When Will said that, it made us sound like horrible, horrid human beings. "Well, whether we win or not, Abby worked really hard on these outfits. I don't want to disappoint her."

He leaned back and rested his arms on the edge of the booth. "I'll take you. No worries." Then he climbed from the booth and walked out of the shop without a backward glance.

Chapter 18

The dress came out exactly as Abby had planned. White netting cascaded around me like a glacier. The underskirt was soft and shimmered. Sequins sewn into the bodice caught the light and glittered.

Abby swept my hair up off my neck, and Erin handed me the prettiest pair of diamond earrings I'd ever seen.

"Those are *yours*?" Abby shrieked when she saw them.

Erin smirked. "You two know so little about me."

Once my transformation was complete, the three of us made a dramatic exit, descending down my stairs as if we were Mary Poppins traveling by fluffy white cloud. When she saw me, my mother began to cry.

My father took pictures, then drove us over to the resort. My dress barely fit into the cab of the truck.

"What's wrong with that kid anyway? You should be picked up. I should be met with." My father was snarling.

"Dad, it's just easier this way," I replied, nudging Abby in her side to stop her laughter. Erin had left us early, to make sure all the decorations in the resort ballroom met with Mean Agnes's approval.

"That kid's just a big softy. Can't even talk to the father of the girl he's dancing with?"

"Dad, I told you, I'm going with Will, not Jake."

My father took his eyes off the road for two seconds to catch my eye. "Oh. In that case, it's all good."

Now Abby's laughter was threatening to spill out of her.

"Dad, that's a double standard."

"No, it's not. I know that kid can take care of himself and therefore can take care of you. I don't think Soft Jake could get himself out of a jam, if you know what I mean."

I didn't, actually, know what he meant.

My father pulled up to the resort and put the gear in park. Then he descended from the cab, came over to my side, and opened the door for me.

"You do look very pretty, honey," he whispered, bending low so I could hear him. "I'm proud of you."

"Thanks, Dad," I whispered back.

"Not too late. If you're not back by eleven, I'm coming in with my shotgun." This, unfortunately, he didn't whisper.

Once he hopped back into his truck and sped off, Abby finally let out her breath. "I don't think that was a joke."

"No," I agreed as I tried to adjust the sleeves of the dress. I was wearing a white faux-fur-lined wrap that Abby had sewn to go with the ensemble, and it was remarkably warm. "You should sell these," I said to her, twirling the cape around so she knew what I was talking about. "It's warmer than Will Parker's coat!"

"Yeah?" Abby grinned. She stood back and admired me. "I can't believe how pretty you are! People are staring!"

I turned from her and for the first time noticed the stream of dressed-up couples pouring through the resort's front gate. And Abby was right. As they walked by, they nodded appreciatively at me.

"You should be really proud." I clutched her hand.

Abby squeezed and prodded me into another twirl. The cape fanned out as I did. "Even if you don't win, I feel really good about this!"

"You should. You should be really, really proud!"

"Wow."

The two of us turned to the sound of the voice, which came from behind Abby. Cam Brock stood near the resort's front entrance with his buddy Jay.

"Whitman, look at you!" Cam exclaimed.

I blushed and put my head down. "Thanks," I said. Abby was suddenly obsessed with my shoes.

"Oh, hey, Abby," Cam said, shoving his hands into his black tuxedo pockets.

There was a moment of silence, so to save us all, I said, "No coat? You cold?"

"Nah," he said. "Like it?" He held out the edges of his jacket to display his threads. Abby kept her head down. My heart was breaking for her.

"Yeah, um, well, we should go inside," I said. "Have you seen Will?"

He gestured to the parking lot. "His truck is here. He's probably inside."

"Okay, well—"

"Yeah, I gotta go pick up—" He shoved his hands back in his pockets, and Jay punched his arm.

"You're lame, man."

"Shut up." He punched him back. Boys had a way of punching each other when they should have been expressing their feelings. Cam had some serious nerve making conversation with us, and the deepening shade of red on Abby's face made me more determined than ever to stomp all over Sabrina's heart by winning this contest.

"Anyway. See you guys. Bye, Ab," he said. She still hadn't looked up. Finally he walked away, around to the parking lot.

She stepped closer to me and clutched my

arm. "I wish he'd forget I existed. It'd be easier that way."

I rubbed her arm in support and then promptly became distracted. There, in the doorway, stood Will Parker, in a black tuxedo jacket and black tie with a white rose in his lapel. His hair looked angelic against the black. His skin was tan. My stomach was on the floor. I chanted a new mantra in my head: *Jake. Jake. Jake.*

He began to walk toward us and then I saw that Erin was with him. She wore a black hooded sweatshirt—the hood was up over her head—and a pair of dark corduroy pants. Her hair was in two long pigtailed braids. When she saw me, she jumped up and down and clapped. "You're pretty!"

"Thanks," I muttered. I was concentrating on restoring my breath. I couldn't remember ever seeing Will in anything other than snow boots or sneakers.

He didn't say anything when he joined our group. Erin looked from him to me and back to him, then nudged my arm. "Okay. Well, do plenty of things I wouldn't do. Come on,

Ab. I'm going to sneak you in through the cafeteria."

Abby grasped my arms as if to hug me, but then just shook me a little. Then the two of them left me and Will out there in the entryway.

He handed me three stalks of lilies. I hadn't noticed that he was holding them. His hand closed over mine when I reached for them. "Here."

"Really?" I asked.

"Really."

"Okay," I said. Suddenly I had an attack of Abby-itis. I couldn't look at him, for some reason, and my stomach felt all flighty again.

With that, he crooked his elbow and held it out for me. "Want to go break some hearts?"

I looked up and seeing him made me smile. I took his arm, and he escorted me inside.

I'd never seen the interior of the resort look like this. Gone were the couches and tables and descending lamps. In place of the normal furniture was a pristine ballroom all in white: white drapes, white settees, white tablecloths.

The lighting was soft, there was a band playing songs — I noticed Jay up there playing bass; he gave us a thumbs-up.

Half of the crowd danced and the other half lounged on a back patio that had been opened and lit up with hundreds of lights. The slopes were lit up too, serving as the most beautiful backdrop imaginable. It looked like something out of a television show.

Will kept hold of my elbow as we walked along the periphery of the room. "Dance or mingle?"

"Um." The thought of dancing with him made my heart speed up. I ground down on my teeth and tried to picture Jake's face.

"I say dance," Will continued, oblivious to my distress. "That way people can get a load of how awesome we look, and maybe they'll drop out of the contest."

"You're devious," I said, smiling.

"Thank you, ma'am." Then he steered me to the floor. Jay gave us another thumbs-up sign, and Will held up his hands as if to tell him to give us a break.

Then the band busted into a slow song. Will swept me into his body and the butterflies in my stomach transformed into full-on flying birds. His hand was on my back, and I couldn't breathe so easy. So I rested my head on his shoulder. From my perch there, I could breathe easier.

"Whitman," Will said, his voice quiet.

"Yeah?" I raised my head and looked him in the eye, and then had to avert my gaze.

"I'm going to spin you a hundred and eighty degrees. Look against the wall."

Sabrina and Cam stood on the outskirts of the floor, not dancing and not looking very happy. In fact Sabrina's arms were crossed and she was glaring in the direction of the dance floor. Will continued to move us in a circle, which was good thinking because it didn't look like I was spying on Sabrina, which, of course, I was. When we rounded back in the proper direction, I realized that she was glaring at us.

"She's angry!" I whisper-shouted.

"Yep. And *I'm* the devious one. You are now officially evil."

I looked back at him. "It's not the costume, you know, it's you."

He looked to Sabrina and then looked at me. "She's not my type."

"I realize that."

His eyebrow went up. "Yeah?"

"Yeah."

Then he spun me around and dipped me. When he brought me back up I laughed. "That'll get her."

"See? Devious."

He shrugged his shoulders. "I have my moments. Besides I'm tired of her. She's not that nice to Cam, and I gotta stick up for my boy."

When we twirled back around, Sabrina and Cam were gone. I spotted them around the corner at a table serving refreshments. She was saying something to him, with her arms crossed and her face contorted. He didn't seem to be paying attention. He ladled a cup of punch and handed it to her. She slammed it down on the table, spun on her heel, and stalked away to where Stephanie and Hannah were conspiring in a corner.

Will continued to twirl me and I continued

to people-watch. "I like being on the floor like this! I can take it all in."

"Yeah, well, I need a break, twinkle toes." Then he dipped me again. I couldn't help myself. I was giggling. He raised me up, and he smiled at me.

We walked to the edge of the room, where Erin and Abby were poking their heads out of a shimmery white curtain.

"You guys are *so* going to win!" Abby squealed.

"Shut up!" Erin poked her in the ribs. "We're going to get nailed for crashing."

Just then a coworker of hers passed us and waved to her. "Hey, Erin!"

"You guys aren't exactly invisible," I said. "Anyone can see you."

"Forget it, then." Erin stepped out from the curtain and pulled Abby out too.

"Did you like my moves?" Will asked Erin.

"You're a regular Fred Astaire," she responded glibly.

"Come on. Dance. I dare you."

Abby and I began chanting, "Do it. Do it."

But just then, a whirlwind of light blue

attacked Will. "Dance with me!" Sabrina shouted.

Will wasn't expecting a full-on assault, so he staggered back from the force of her hug. Once he realized what was happening, he peeled her hands from around his neck and pushed her away. "Sabrina, hey."

Sabrina didn't even look at the three of us girls. "Will. Dance with me," she commanded.

Will, for once, was a little speechless.

Erin, as ever, was not. "Sorry, Sabrina. He's with us."

Erin removed the hood from her head, shot us a look, and walked to the middle of the dance floor, where she held out her arm as she waited for Will to join her.

He ran to her.

Sabrina's face turned twelve shades of red. I thought she might cry. Then she spun on her heel and stalked off to the girls' room.

"I can't believe her. She's going to get fired!" Abby gushed as we watched Erin on the dance floor.

"A little fun will do her good," I responded.

Will spun her around, and Erin laughed

while she danced. It was nice to see her so smiley, and I realized that Will probably had thought the same thing, which was why he had asked her to dance in the first place.

"Oh!"

"What?"

"Huh?"

"You said 'Oh' out loud."

"I did?"

"Yeah. You did."

I didn't know how to put into words what I had just realized. How to explain a moment that has no rhyme or reason to it? But watching Will Parker in a suit, knowing he was doing me a favor, watching him goad Erin into smiles, for the first time I had a real notion that he *did* care about some things.

But luckily I didn't have to explain this to Abby, because at that moment, Cam Brock appeared before us. His face was ashen and his hands were in his pockets like they always were. "Hey, Abby," he said.

"You want something to drink?" she asked me. "I'm going to get something to drink." And then she tried to walk away, but Cam reached out and grabbed her arm. This surprised her. And me.

"Sorry," he said, letting her go.

"I'll get it," I said. "Drinks all around." Abby's face looked petrified at the notion of being left alone with him, but it seemed fairly clear to me that he wanted to talk to her.

As I walked to the refreshment table, I turned to spy on them, to make sure that our poor Abby was holding her own. What I saw shocked me. He was leading her to the dance floor! Her face looked dazed, but happy. Then Erin waved her arm in the air, which caught my attention. Once we locked eyes, she pointed at Cam and Abby and made a happy face.

I poured myself a glass of punch. It was red and sticky and sweet. As I drank, I watched my two best friends, dressed in casual black clothes, infiltrating the dance floor and having a wonderful time.

Chapter 19

$\mathcal{A}$fter the winners of the Annual Best Costume Contest were announced, the entire party was ushered outside, where the party organizers had transformed the walkway to the main chairlift into a path of lights. There were candles everywhere, on the path itself and hanging from the bare tree branches. Once we were all outside, Mean Agnes gave an order and the entire resort powered down. All the electric lights were shut off, and the whole area fell into a hushed quiet.

The group of us huddled near a large tree, and peered up into the night searching for the natural light show. Unfortunately there were too many clouds to make it worthwhile.

"It's freezing out here!" I exclaimed, as I wrapped the cape tightly around me and blew out a stream of breathy air.

"I thought your sash would keep you warm," Erin wisecracked.

I felt across my chest for the Best Costume sash. "It does! It does!"

Abby jumped up and down and clapped. "I can't believe it! We won!" She fingered the sash that she was wearing—as soon as Will and I were handed the winning title, he had given his sash to Abby and told her she deserved it. It was a really nice thing for him to do.

So now, the dance was at its end, and Abby and I were in matching sashes, though mine was over layers of white lace and hers was over a black sweatshirt. But that wasn't the source of her giddy happiness. No, the source was approaching us with a handful of paper cups.

"Here, this'll keep you warm," Cam said, handing each of us girls a steaming hot chocolate.

"Thanks," Abby said shyly. Erin's smile was bigger than I'd ever seen it.

It turned out that our goal of seeing Sabrina Hartley in tears was achieved, but it had nothing to do with our costumes. In fact, Cam and

Sabrina had gotten in a spat almost as soon as they'd arrived, and Cam had finally told her that she had to be nicer or he was going to break up with her.

Well, Sabrina is a lot of things, but naturally nice isn't one of them. That was when she had marched over to Will and thrown herself at him. Soon after, Cam had asked Abby to dance. And the rest of the night, he'd spent with her.

I'd never seen her look so happy.

"Too bad there are so many clouds tonight," Erin said wistfully.

"Yeah, I'd wanted to see the northern lights," Abby agreed.

"Ah, it's cold anyway. Diner anyone?" Cam asked.

A half hour later, the five of us were crammed into the corner booth at the Mountain Diner, in what I had always thought of as Sabrina's booth.

Cam's arm was around Abby's shoulders, and Erin was eating the biggest plate of French fries I'd ever seen.

Will sat next to me, leaning across to pick off of Erin's plate. He was describing what it was like to be assaulted by Sabrina.

"I thought my life was ending in a flash of blue satin."

"Seriously, what was I thinking?" Cam asked. Abby blushed.

I leaned into the booth and caught myself feeling content. I had had a really good time at the ball, with my two best friends and Will and Cam. I ate a fry, feeling slightly guilty about enjoying myself so much when my boyfriend was sitting home alone. I knew that I should leave, call Jake, and go back to my real life.

Will nudged me in my side. "Come back, Whitman. Where's your mind at?"

"School," I lied without thinking.

There was a collective groan at the table. Erin threw a fry at me. "Don't talk about that!"

"Hey!" Abby squealed. "Don't throw food at my creation!"

Just then, as if he could hear my thoughts, Jake appeared at our table. I held my breath. Everyone went quiet, especially Will. Erin kicked me beneath the table.

"Hey!" I finally greeted him. "Look." I held out the sash for him to see. "We won!"

Jake tried to read the writing on it. "Oh," he said, confused. "What'd you win?"

Erin found her voice. "They won Best Costume. Abby made them. For Jessie and Will."

The table had already been quiet, but this brought it down even further.

"Here, sit down," Will said finally. He squeezed in closer to me to make room for Jake, but Erin, who was on my other side, refused to budge. This caused me to be squished.

"Watch the dress!" Abby scolded.

"Let me out," I said quietly to Will.

His face fell. "No, just—don't go yet."

"Come on, Jessie." Jake held out his hand for me.

"I have to. Just move," I said to Will.

Will slid out of the booth so I could follow suit. When I stood up, I presented the skirt to Jake so he could see. "See? Best Costume. Abby rules."

Jake didn't really say anything. He reached for my hand and turned to the table. "See you guys later."

Everybody mumbled good-byes to me,

except for Erin and Will. As Jake and I walked out of the door, I turned to catch a last glimpse of them. Will stared at me. I smiled but he didn't smile back.

Jake walked me home while I tried to stop myself from thinking about Will so much.

"Was it fun?" he asked as we passed the turnoff to Mr. Winter's farm.

I didn't answer right away. What was I supposed to say? Was I supposed to tell him that I had had a great time, and that it had been great because I'd been with Will? I was starting to seriously hate myself. "Yes," I answered after a moment. "It was fun. I think Cam and Sabrina broke up for good."

"Sabrina's the girl you hate, right?"

"I don't *hate* her," I grumbled.

Jake laughed. "Okay. I'm not even sure if I know which one she is, but I know you hate her."

This made me feel even worse, so this time I didn't say anything. I focused on how cold my ears and hands were. Also, I couldn't feel my toes anymore. These shoes were pretty, but they pinched the front of my feet, and they weren't exactly built to keep out the snow. I thought about how nice it would be to still be at the diner, with my friends, laughing at Will's stories of Sabrina and thinking about what a good dancer he was. About how funny he'd been on the dance floor, dipping me so close to the ground that I could've kissed it.

"What's so funny?" Jake asked me.

I looked at him, surprised that I had been smiling broadly enough for him to see it in the night's darkness.

"Nothing. Just thinking about accepting my crown," I lied again. As soon as the words were out of my mouth, my spirits plummeted. Why was I telling lies? I just wanted to get home.

But when we finally arrived at my house, the awkward feeling I had increased.

"Want to hang out a little bit?" Jake asked me, when we got to the doorway.

"No, it's too late. My dad will freak."

Jake's brows moved toward the middle of his face. He was surprised that I had said no. In fact, I was surprised that I had said no. It *wasn't* too late. If it had been Will who'd walked me home, my dad would've invited him in. This thought made me feel even grumpier, so I kissed Jake on the cheek and sent him home.

Later, once I was back in my room, and taking the dress off, and removing the pins from my hair, and sitting on my bed with Teddy on my lap, all I could think about was Will. How handsome he looked. How sweet he was to Erin. How fun it was to dance with him. How close he sat next to me in the booth.

I thought too about English class, about what it would be like to see him in the halls of Willow High. I hugged Teddy more tightly. I realized that no matter what I did to try to keep myself from liking Will, when we got back to school I would always be looking for him in the halls, just like all the other girls there did.

It was all Will's fault. He'd gone and cast his stupid spell on me, and I hadn't been strong enough to keep it from happening. And this dance was the last time I'd ever have any time with him. And I hadn't realized until this moment that I felt *sad* about it.

The worst thing was that I had been disappointed to see Jake at the diner and that shouldn't be how a girl felt to see her boyfriend. I was beginning to feel really bad about myself. Here I'd used Will to get Jake, I'd manipulated everybody until Jake had broken up with Evie, and now I was sitting alone, having gotten everything I'd wanted, and I didn't want it anymore.

I had become Sabrina.

I wondered if it was too late to make myself a big Cheer-up Shake.

Chapter 20

*W*hen I opened my eyes the next morning, they focused almost immediately on the winner's sash, which I had thumbtacked to my wall the night before. Sitting up, I read the words BEST COSTUME, then immediately closed my eyes.

The feelings I had had the night before came rushing back: the knotty stomach and the pounding heartbeat that all spoke to the fact that I felt guilty.

I bounded out of bed, showered, and brushed my hair. When I got to the kitchen with a notion that I'd try to choke down some cereal, Brian was at the table, his head in his hands, his face glum, and his blueberry muffin in a thousand little pieces as if he had smashed it.

Normally I would've eaten my cereal and ignored him. But the *guilt* I felt was all-consuming and I was desperate to make it go away. I knew the only way to do that was to start at least acting like a good-hearted person. Hopefully I could fake the goodness until I made it. "What's up?" I asked him.

He didn't seem surprised by my concern at all. In fact, he didn't even look up or answer me.

So I started again, pulling out a chair and sitting next to him. "Wanna go skiing today? I'll take you. We can even go get your little friend if you want." I swallowed a bit of cereal and noticed that my chest already felt a bit less edgy. Good deeds were good medicine.

Brian didn't seem as high on my offer as I was. He balled his hand into a fist and brought it down on the smashed-up muffin, causing it to crumble into a million more pieces.

"Okay," I said, trying to figure out his problem. "Skating then?"

"Whatever," he replied, his head in his hands, sounding sadder than ever.

"Brian, what's going on?"

He finally raised his eyes. "Will you help me write a letter?"

I spent the rest of my morning sitting by

the computer, helping my brother compose an email that would make any twelve-year-old proud. It turned out that he was feeling blue because Tiffany had left early with her father and Evie. I had been so caught up in my own plans, I hadn't realized that she had left too. As I thought about it, Brian hadn't been in my way at all the past couple of days. He'd been sad for days and I hadn't even noticed. There was no two ways about it: I had to try to be a better sister.

When we'd finally come up with something he felt good about, we hit SEND, and he turned to me, grinning. He hopped off the chair, kicked me in the shin, and then ran into the living room where he promptly began playing video games. I screamed in pain and muttered something about getting him back, before remembering my vow of only a few moments before to be a better sister. Maybe being a better sister meant understanding that a kick in the shin from Brian wasn't really a kick in the shin. Maybe in Brian's world, it was a proper thank-you. It was funny to me that he was at his most destructive when he felt his best.

I turned to the computer, looking at the message confirming delivery of his email, thinking to myself that maybe Tiffany was going to be to Brian what Jake had been to me. A source of happiness that had nothing to do with our daily routines.

I scooted closer to the monitor and poised my fingers over the keys. I knew I had to do something. I owed Evie an apology, and I really should've done it in person. I had single-handedly ruined this girl's vacation. No amount of Cheer-up Shakes could take that feeling away.

I worked on my email for a half hour. I told her that it had been really nice to meet her, and that when her family came back to Willow Hill, Erin, Abby, and I would be excited to see her and would help her with her skiing skills. And then I apologized if the vacation hadn't been what she'd expected this year. I didn't come right out and say anything about Jake, but I hoped she'd understand that I knew I had done wrong.

After I finished the email, I pulled on Will's coat, covered my face and hands and head in as many layers as I could, and trudged over to Snow Cones. The place was nearly empty when I got there, and I occupied my time by making Apology Sundaes (vanilla ice cream, chopped-up Snickers bars, and caramel sauce). I made three of them, and put them in paper cups with plastic lids. Packing them into a paper bag, I headed out to make amends.

I'd always avoided Sabrina Hartley, so actually seeking her out made me feel like I was in the Twilight Zone. I first tried the tanning place in the middle of town, then the Mountain Diner, and then the spa area at the resort. She was nowhere to be found.

I walked the trails behind the skiing hills, then went to the skating area, and finally ended up back at Erin's post in the lodge.

"You're looking for who?" Her eyes were wide in disbelief.

"I'm making amends," I pronounced.

"*You're* making amends to *her*?" She dropped her book onto the counter and it fluttered closed.

"Your place!" I exclaimed, imagining how

upset I'd be to lose my place in a thousand-page book.

"Nah. I'm finished."

"Good?" I asked.

"Very." Erin straightened her back and reached for me. "While I think you're crazy, I hope that you're going to set *everything* right."

I took a breath. I had a feeling that she meant Will.

She continued on, "I just mean that you shouldn't assume that because a guy is nice and funny and charming that he doesn't *mean* it."

I nodded and showed her the contents of the paper bag I was carrying. "See the largest ice-cream cup in there? That's for Will."

I found Sabrina at Mr. Winter's. She, Stephanie, and Hannah stood in the pen, their feet being attacked by six little bundles of fluff.

As I walked toward them, Stephanie nudged Sabrina in the side to alert her to the fact that I was approaching. When she saw me, her face fell. Even the dogs sensed that something was up, because all of them except for one scattered away. Sabrina scooped up the pup that remained by her feet and cuddled him to her face as I kept walking. The sight of her hugging the dog reminded me of how I'd clutch Teddy when I needed some support.

Since I was confronting the three goons, I decided that an overt apology might cause them to gang up on me. You never knew what would set off a gaggle of high school girls. Then I realized that I had *three* ice-cream sundaes with me.

"Hey, guys," I said, my voice sounding a little froggy.

They didn't respond. Stephanie narrowed her eyes at me in a clear sign of disapproval over the coat I was wearing.

I swallowed and gathered my courage. "Sabrina, I didn't get a chance to tell you that I thought your dress last night was spectacular."

Now they were looking at me like I was an alien being or something. But no matter, I plunged ahead.

"Here." I thrust the bag at them. "I made

you all some ice-cream sundaes."

Sabrina looked cautiously at the other girls before extending a tentative hand and taking the bag from me.

"Are you trying to poison me or something?" she finally asked.

"Oh gosh, no!" I continued on bravely. "If I used my mother's ice cream as a murder weapon, she'd never let me out of the house again."

I noticed that Hannah smiled a little, which bolstered my courage. "I just thought, you know, the break was almost over, and that we all needed something to enjoy before school started up again. So, you know. That's it."

After a silent few moments, I figured they didn't know what to make of me and my gifts. Finally I realized that I couldn't make it any more normal by staring at them. "Well, see you guys around." I waved and headed back the way I came.

"Hey," I heard Sabrina call out to me.

When I turned around, she said, "Congrats on the Best Costume thing. You totally deserved it."

I smiled. "Thanks!"

She nodded. "Tell Abby I said the clothes were perfect."

I had to go back to Snow Cones to make two more Apology Sundaes. When I got there, Jake was waiting at the counter. He was wearing a dark-green, crewneck sweater and khaki pants. My heart started pounding. Knowing what I had to do made me nervous and sad. I'd never broken up with anyone before. I suddenly sympathized with him for avoiding breaking up with me in person. It wasn't fun *at all*.

I walked behind the counter and began filling a dish with ingredients as he sat and watched me work. His expression was one of suspicion.

We didn't say much until I'd finished and slid the metal dish to him. When he caught my eye, I could see by the sadness in his face that he knew what was about to happen.

"Jake, I—"

"Just don't say it, okay?"

"Okay."

"What's this one?" He lifted his spoon and dipped it into the ice cream. His shy smile caused the dimples in his cheeks to reveal themselves. He was so completely cute, and yet, I knew very well that my stomach had zero butterflies in it.

"Apology Sundae," I said matter-of-factly.

He took a bite. "What's the key component of saying 'I'm sorry'?"

"Vanilla ice cream."

He laughed a bit. "I thought you were going to say the Snickers bars."

"Nah," I said. "The Snickers are there to make the apology go down easy."

He placed his spoon on the table. "Should I apologize first or you?"

I leaned over and patted his hand. "Maybe we should apologize at the same time."

"Okay. One, two, three—"

We each said, "I'm sorry," and then I laughed and squeezed his hand.

"We're leaving tomorrow."

"I know," I said to him.

"I'm really sorry about everything."

"Just eat your ice cream."

That left one dish of ice cream for me to give, but when it came time for me to put it together, I decided that an Apology Sundae wasn't the right approach. When I finally made a shake that said exactly what I wanted to say, I set off. This time I knew exactly where to go. I didn't need Erin or anybody to guide me to Mount Crow.

At first, Will was a speck at the top of the mountain, but I knew it was him. Nobody in town could leap into the air as high as he could, and the navy suit was a dead giveaway. There were a few people at the bottom of the mountain near where I was standing who cheered and whooped watching his display, and I couldn't help but feel proud of him. He deserved people's cheers. He was good at what he did.

He didn't see me when he got to the bottom of the mountain. I supposed that it was his white coat I was wearing. It *did* blend into the scenery.

"Will!" I called out.

He turned at the sound of my voice and when he saw it was me, his face split into a grin and he ripped his goggles off of his face. His cheeks were vibrantly red from the exertion. His head was covered in a navy knit cap, and from the moment he looked at me, there were flocks of butterflies alight in my stomach. I felt my face burst into a smile.

He was taken aback by my happy exterior and scrunched his face up at me. "You just break Sabrina's legs or something?"

I shook my head. "Just happy to see you." It was the most honest thing I'd ever said in my whole life.

He snapped his feet from his board, kicked it up so that he could catch it with his left hand, and stepped closer to me. For once, he seemed speechless, so I thrust the large paper cup at him. I'd put a red straw in it.

"I didn't realize you delivered," he said.

"For my very special customers."

"Are you going to tell me what it is?"

I raised my shoulders and dropped them. "I

think you have to find out for yourself."

"I accept your challenge," he said before taking a long sip.

"Good?" I asked eagerly.

"Delicious," he concluded. "What is it?"

I took a step closer to him. "*That* is the new-and-improved, absolutely authentic Jessie Whitman Love Shake."

His eyebrows shot up and I lowered my head in a fit of shyness. For a moment, I didn't know who I thought I was!

Then he reached forward, picked up my hand, and pulled me forward so that we were standing very close to each other. He said softly, "Just for me?"

I raised my eyes to meet his and said, "Only for you."

He looked into my eyes for a moment and then lifted the cup to me. "Let's share it."

I took a sip of the shake, and smiled at him before being overcome by a severe case of embarrassment. I lowered my head and he reached around to hug me. I finally found my voice, which wasn't easy to do since my insides were so alive with happiness. "So I thought I'd hang on to your coat for a while."

He leaned his forehead into mine, and said, "I wouldn't have my girl wearing anything else. Come on, let's get you a snowboard."

He led me to the lodge, and as he did, I looked up into the sky and thought that there was nowhere I'd rather be.

Cozy up to another fun winter romance with
SUITE DREAMS by Rachel Hawthorne

School's out for the holidays . . . but the fun has just begun!

Sometimes a twist of fate leads you to love.

"So what are you and the main squeeze doing over winter break?"

We were definitely not going to do any squeezing. Although I wasn't ready to admit that yet. Not to anyone. Not even Mel, the closest thing I had to a best friend on campus.

It was a little after eleven and we were walking home after finishing our shift at The Chalet—a fancy schmancy restaurant near the university where we were both students.

Mel was a year older than I was, but she didn't hold my freshman status against me. Besides, after only one semester I was a mere three hours short of being a sophomore myself, having placed out of some courses and then carrying a full course load.

I was embarrassingly smart—at least in the world of academia.

When it came to relationships with guys,

though, I was a total ignoramus.

Case in point: Today was the beginning of winter break and my first boyfriend ever was at that very moment flying the friendly skies, heading to Australia.

I'd met Rick the day I moved into Wilson Hall. He'd helped unload my boxes from my parents' car, teasing me the entire time because I had so much stuff. He was a minimalist, who boasted that he could fit his life into one box. He'd never met a single-purpose item that he liked.

We'd spent the semester hanging out together, being a couple. We lived in the same co-ed dorm, which made it convenient. We ate meals together, went to the library to study, attended football games, and had amazing make-out sessions.

I'd viewed the upcoming winter break — when studying wasn't a necessity — as a time for us to take our relationship to the next level, to strengthen our bond, to get to know each other even better. In retrospect, I suppose you should know someone well before you jump into a relationship, and a guy's box-hauling skills may not be the best indicator for judging your compatibility. Even if he is cute with a slow-to-curl-up sexy smile.

But right before finals, we'd begun to question whether or not we were really working as a couple. We'd hugged, I'd cried, we'd both admitted that *something* was missing. But what exactly? We didn't know. So we'd decided to take a break from each other. We'd stay friends. Maybe we'd get back together—maybe not.

The timing of our decision couldn't have been worse. I'd thought we were going to spend winter break together so I'd told my parents that I was staying on campus. By the time I realized I would be among only a handful of students who stayed *and* I'd be without Rick, my parents had already packed up and headed for warmer climes.

Yeah, sure, it wasn't too late for me to meet up with them somewhere, but let's get real here. Would you want to spend your winter break constantly within nine yards of your parents?

Me either. I love them, but the love deepens at a distance.

So I was staying on campus as originally

planned. I was just doing it without Rick.

"Oh, no," Mel said, suddenly taking my arm and turning me toward her. "I know that look. Alyssa, did you guys break up?"

"What? No. Absolutely not." I felt as though I was in a Shakespeare play, protesting too much and hoping she wouldn't notice. Rick and I had agreed not to tell anyone, just in case we got back together. It would be less awkward around our friends that way. "It's just that, well, he went to Australia."

Her hazel eyes widened at that news. "Wow! What'd he do? Come into an inheritance?"

I actually laughed. Mel had that effect on me. She made things seem not quite so dire and unmanageable. "No, at least I don't think so. He discovered couch surfing. People let strangers sleep on their couch, and then they go sleep on someone else's couch."

"*Ew!* Sounds a little too *Hostel* for me. Does he even know these people?"

I'd worried about that, too. "He said it was safe. He used an Internet site. People are interviewed or something. I'm not really sure how it all works."

"So how long is Rick gonna be gone?" she asked.

"Until the next semester starts."

"Bummer."

I supposed that I could talk to Mel, get her opinion on things, but it wasn't as though we'd done any deep soul sharing. We'd bonded over spilled drinks, bitchy customers, and taking up the slack at each other's tables. But we weren't to the point where we could talk about anything and everything.

"That's four weeks of dateless-ness," Mel continued. "What are you going to do?"

"Take a couple of classes over the mini-mester. Maybe work some extra hours."

"Omigod! Classes and work over winter break? Are you crazy?"

"But I want to do it. And with Rick gone, I'm looking at empty hours."

"Okay, but before classes start on Monday, you need to do something totally wild. We'll go to the lodge and have a spa day."

My parents *had* sent me some extra money so I could enjoy myself over winter break. I nodded, decision made. "Okay. Let's do it."

"Great! And I'll request a male massage therapist. They have such strong hands."

I think she actually shivered and I didn't think it was from the cold. We reached the edge of campus where our paths diverged.

"Have sweet dreams about Hans with the magic hands," she said.

Laughing, I watched as she hurried down the street toward a house she rented with some other students. As a sophomore she wasn't restricted to living on campus, like I was.

Because the town had a low crime rate, I felt comfortable walking on alone, even though it was so late. Besides, I carried pepper spray in my jacket pocket. My dad had given it to me when I left for college.

The wind picked up. Snow was falling more heavily.

As I approached Wilson Hall, I couldn't help but think it looked deserted. It was more of a residential house than a typical dorm. It had four floors, each floor had several suites. Very quaint and cozy.

I turned up the short walkway that led to the front steps. Out of the corner of my eye I saw someone—large and broad—lurch out from the shadows at the side of the house. Startled, I stepped back, blinking rapidly against the fat snowflakes that were hampering my visibility. The only things that registered were that I didn't know him, he was moving fast, and he looked to have the power of a bulldozer. With survival reflexes kicking in, I yanked the pepper spray out of my jacket pocket, I sprayed him in the face before darting past him—

"What the f—" His curses were muffled because he dropped to the ground and face-planted in the snow.

Then I heard, "What'd you do that for?"

The guy sounded completely baffled instead of angry or mean. But more intriguing, he spoke with an Australian accent. I was a sucker for accents. I looked back over my shoulder. The guy had straightened and was kneeling with his snow-filled hands cupped over his eyes. Keeping my finger poised on the pepper spray nozzle, I crept slowly toward the edge of the porch. "Who are you?"

My voice sounded all high and squeaky. Maybe because I was close to hyperventilating.

"Jude. Jude Hawkins." He'd pushed the gravelly words out through clenched teeth. "Dammit! It hurts like the devil."

He sounded as though he was in serious pain. Guilt shot through me. I glanced around. He was alone, but the question remained—

"Why, why are you here?" I demanded, grateful to sound a little more in control and less like air leaking out of a balloon.

He scooped up more snow, dropped his head back, and put the icepack-fashioned mounds over his eyes. "How long is it gonna sting?"

He appeared fairly harmless now, which was the whole point of pepper spray, I guessed. Still I felt badly that I'd reacted first and was asking questions later. "I'm not sure. About half an hour or so, maybe longer."

He groaned, and if at all possible his groan carried an Australian accent.

"I'm really sorry, but—*what* are you doing out here? I mean it's late and you were lurking in the shadows—"

"I wasn't lurking. I was staying out of the wind and snow, waiting for someone to come along and let me in. The door's locked."

"Yeah, they're keeping it locked over winter break," I said. "Do you know someone who's living here? Is there someone I should get for you?"

"All I need is the couch."

"The couch?"

"Yeah. A bloke swapped couches with me."

Okay, a sneaky suspicion began working its way through my locked-down brain. I didn't think he was bringing in a couch and taking one out. I didn't think he was talking about that kind of swapping. "Uh, who offered you a couch?"

"Bloke named Rick. Rick Whirly. You know him?"

"Um, yeah." Had he offered Jude the couch in his suite in exchange for a couch in Australia? Was that how this couch surfing thing worked? I didn't have a clue. I sank down into the snow. "I am *so* sorry."

With his gloved hands, he brushed the snow off his face and squinted at me. "Are you Alyssa Manning?"

"How did you know—"

"He mentioned you."

"Unfortunately he didn't tell me about you," I confessed.

"Huh. That's odd."

Actually, it wasn't. Part of the reason behind our taking a break from each other was that I wanted communication between us. Rick thought kissing was communication. And okay, on some level it was, but I wanted words as well.

Reaching out, I wrapped my hand around Jude's arm. "Come on. Let's get inside so I can look at the damage. Blink as fast as you can. I read somewhere it helps. Creates a natural wash like eye drops, or something." I was babbling as I pulled him up to his feet.

"What *was* that anyway?" he asked, and his sexy accent made me wish *he* was the one doing the babbling.

"Pepper spray," I reluctantly confessed.

"That's illegal in Australia."

"Yeah, it is in some states here, too." I wasn't sure about Vermont. I guessed I'd find out if he brought charges against me.

Jude stumbled—

"Whoa!" I cried, grabbing him, trying to stop his fall.

But he was way bigger than I was. We

tumbled sideways off the walk onto the snow-covered ground with a *whump*, Jude sprawled on top of me.

The distant streetlights and moonlight cast a faint glow over us. Jude was blinking, squinting, his face scrunched up. But even all scrunched, he was too cute for words. I was really wishing we'd started this encounter totally differently — like without me coming off as psycho-crazed girl.

"Sorry about that," Jude said.

I felt this odd sort of excitement, like waiting for the first burst of fireworks on New Year's Eve. It was strange. We weren't doing anything and yet anticipation sparked through me. It was weird. I'd never felt this way with Rick.

The snow was beginning to melt through my black pants. As much as I hated to end this moment of having a hunk so near —

"Uh, you know what? We can get inside more quickly if you get off me," I told Jude.

"Oh, right, sorry. I can barely think through this hideous pain."

"Is it really that bad?" I asked, horrified at the thought.

"Nah, my eyes are just feeling like they're on fire now. Before I thought they'd been nuked." He rolled awkwardly off me, as though he was groping to figure out where he was. "I hope I'm not gonna go blind. Wouldn't that be a jolly good beginning to a holiday?"

"It's not supposed to cause any permanent damage," I said. At least I didn't think it was.

Taking hold of his arm again, I led him up the steps and across the porch to the door.

I guided the wounded Aussie to the kitchen.

"Here, sit down." I pulled out a chair.

He sat with a thud.

Jude pulled off his knit cap. He had brown hair that had streaks of blond and reddish gold running through it. It reminded me of the autumn leaves I enjoyed so much. The skin around his eyes was blotchy. Guilt once again prickled through me. "I read somewhere that milk will ease the sting."

"I really don't think washing my face with milk is the way to go here." He blinked several times. "They're feeling better, to be honest. I think the blinking helped." He nodded. "Yeah, I think it's gonna be okay."

If not having any white in your eyes was okay. They were seriously bloodshot. If not for the redness, Jude's eyes might have been the most beautiful I'd ever seen. They were an emerald green, deep and velvety looking.

"You're prettier than your picture," Jude said.

I realized he'd been studying me as closely as I was him. I felt the heat rush to my cheeks. "My picture?"

"Yeah, Rick sent me a picture of you. You know. We exchanged photos, tried to bridge the thousands of miles that separated us."

"What did he say about me?" I asked, genuinely curious.

"I can show you."

He unzipped an outer pocket on his jacket, reached inside, and pulled out a piece of paper. He unfolded it and handed it to me.

It was an email from Rick.

Hello, mate! LOL. I'm practicing my Australian. How am I doing? I'll be crashing on your couch by the time you crash on mine but don't worry. If you run into any problems, just find Alyssa. She'll take care of them, whatever they are. She can show you around, find you some cheap eats, make sure you have a good time. Whatever you need, just ask her. She's all about being there for others.

Your couch-swapping mate,
Rick

I lifted my gaze to Jude. He was still grinning, as though everything was going to be okay. Problem-solver Alyssa was on the job. I felt as though I needed a superhero costume with a cape and a big P on the front or something.

Thanks, Rick. Thanks a lot. Might have been nice to tell me you were volunteering me to be a one-person welcoming committee to a hot Aussie!